Howard Seely

A Lone Star Bo-Peep, and Other Tales of Texan Ranch Life

Howard Seely

A Lone Star Bo-Peep, and Other Tales of Texan Ranch Life

ISBN/EAN: 9783337034061

Printed in Europe, USA, Canada, Australia, Japan

Cover: Foto ©Andreas Hilbeck / pixelio.de

More available books at **www.hansebooks.com**

A LONE STAR BO-PEEP

AND

OTHER TALES

OF

TEXAN RANCH LIFE

BY

HOWARD SEELY

———

NEW YORK:
W. L. MERSHON & CO.
1885.

W. L. Mershon & Co.,
Printers, Electrotypers and Binders,
Rahway, N. J.

TO

ANDREW F. UNDERHILL,

IN TESTIMONY

OF

A FRIENDSHIP OF YEARS.

CONTENTS.

A LONE STAR BO-PEEP.

—o—

I.

DAY was just breaking on the Chadbourne Trail. The pale mists, surprised by rosy Aurora, were scampering in hurried dishabille across its wavering outline, tearing their trailing night-robes upon the thorny mesquites and scattering filmy draperies in its live oak aisles. A few faint stars, through fleecy cloud-rifts, still twinkled tearfully, and but a moment ago the waning moon, that had languished in the western heaven, had lain a pale face upon the sloping shoulder of a great divide and wearily sunk to rest within its somber bosom. There is a dewy freshness in the air; a strong, damp, earthy odor; then on the wings of a gentle breeze—fragrant forerunner of morning—the scent of a thousand wild-flowers swinging their perfumed censers in worship of the coming sun.

Meanwhile, in the shadowy vistas of the dim shrubbery, vague, indistinct forms seem moving. They flit to and fro with a skulking and stealthy movement ; they seem alert, uneasy, restless— the ghosts of incarnate suspicion. Suddenly they are off in a body with a precipitate haste that is ludicrous in its apparent cowardice.

Immediately and sharply to the right comes a quick, startled sound like that made by a stone shaken violently in some metal vessel. The sounds increase and seem associated with the movement of some impeded and lumbering animal. An oath ! a shot ! The sulphurous suggestion of man and gunpowder ! While after a silence more apparent from the recent explosion, during which the rising orb comes proudly up the horizon, a large pecan motte, now visible, and from which the recent disturb ances have proceeded, resounds with shrieks and barks, as if all Bedlam were let loose—the impotent cries of Texan *coyotes*. They die away down the wind. The silence now and the sunlight hold sway.

Within the still, dim precincts of this motte,

the skeleton of a denuded cow-pen stretches its emaciate length. A cooking-stove, lidless, doorless, broken-legged, stares with uncompromising effrontery at the encroaching light. Garments that have survived their usefulness, scattered here and there, like uniforms of the fallen, lend their additional aid to the general air of discomfiture. Civilization seems to have encountered Nature and suffered defeat. Thus desolate, since a remote " round-up," has this live-stock Andersonville remained. It was left for Mr. Faye Howe to revisit its belligerent remindings and speculate upon its analogies.

I am not over-confident that the gentleman was alive to these. Mr. Howe was out of humor. Mr. Howe was sleepy. The languor of disturbed dreams clouded his otherwise acute perceptions. At the precise moment that he dawns upon the reader's consciousness, his bearing is unobservant, his attitude unconsidered. The details of his bivouac are in a sense martial, without its vigilance. Enveloped in his gray blanket and with his head in the hollow of his saddle, he appears lost in the embraces of the drowsy god. But the presence of his recently discharged revolver, and at

a few yards' distance the already stiffening carcass of **a** coyote betray evidences of recently
aroused energy. The only object **at** present
gifted with volition, however, seems his belled
and hoppled light sorrel—from certain "cold
gravy" resemblances denominated "Oscar
Wilde"—Mr. **Howe's** remote and sarcastic protest against England's sufficiently recent inflic-
tion. **Mr.** Faye Howe is an American, and does
not consider his country or its government a necessarily dangerous experiment. **He is** as yet
serenely unaware that he can derive any enlight-
enment political from the "other side." Mr.
Faye **Howe** is not **a** snob ; he **is not a** toady.
Mr. **Faye** Howe **is,** nevertheless, between
twenty-six and twenty-seven.

For the next hour **or** so the neighboring solitude suffers little change. The hampered mustang with its unmelodious accompaniment pur-
sues the ancient and equine occupation **of**
Nebuchadnezzar **with an** occasional snort of
satisfaction. A peripatetic chaparral-cock, with
the unexplainable weakness **of that** bird for
morning calls, had perched upon a pinnacle of
the neighboring cow-pen, and, turning his wise
head **upon one side,** speculated for some min-

utes with gratuitous gravity and the air of a puzzled physician, upon the laziness of his extemporized patient; and then departed upon his customary rounds. In the meantime, the beams of the long arisen sun shot through the branches of the overhanging pecans and heated the blonde head of the sleeper uncomfortably. He turned uneasily. Later several acute twinges made him conscious that he was an obstacle to a caravan of pilgrim ants, which held their inflexible line of march across his recumbent body. He rose to a sitting posture with significant haste. Still heavy with the dews of sleep, Mr. Howe became nevertheless aware of a pattering, clicking sound, made by successive objects dropping from the surrounding air. Staggering to his feet, he instinctively sought the carcass of the dead coyote. It was covered with the already present and constantly arriving hosts of the burying beetle. A grim, flapping shadow intruded itself for a second upon its sun-steeped outline. He raised his eyes. A turkey-buzzard with gory crest looked down in ghoul-like sedateness from a limb above. The speedy burial service of Southern latitudes was already in progress.

With a dejection of manner, aggravated, no
doubt, by an empty stomach, Howe busied
himself in the preparation of a primitive
repast. An adjacent pool of water, of which
the encircling pecans were an infallible index,
assisted him in hasty ablutions—somewhat perfunctory under the circumstances. Refreshed
by these sketchy efforts, he rekindled the embers of his dying fire, cut a forked stick of the
mesquite, and toasted some strips of bacon
from a piece tied up in a sack behind his saddle.
The odor of the broiling morsels stimulated an
appetite already whetted by the balsamic air
of the wilds. With the aid of a loaf of bread,
and some cool water dipped from the neighboring pool with the brim of his sombrero, he
accomplished a hearty—because hungry—repast. The completion of this meal, the observant buzzard, now reinforced by several contemplative comrades, awaited with a patient etiquette which his presence enforced. Then
saddling, with incongruous haste, his satirically
entitled steed, this solitary wayfarer sprang
into his stirrups, and rode carelessly away from
his sylvan bed-chamber and breakfast-room,
without even a casual survey of what he left
behind him.

II.

AS Mr. Howe emerged from the shelter of the pecan motte, and rode out upon the plain, a sense of exuberant health made him bestride his muscular horse with a feeling of elation. A short ride brought him to the line of the Trail, into which he at once turned, and for a few moments pursued his way between its mesquite fringes with preoccupied thoughtfulness. Doubtless few of his whilom companions would have recognized in this sun-tanned and centaur-riding wanderer a certain aspirant for collegiate honors of a few years previous. Yet such *was* he. A critical inspection developed the fact that his garments—albeit conventional and of the traditional type—did not set upon him with the habitude of a frontiersman. Aside from their newness, there was a lack of intimacy between them and the limbs of their wearer which at once obtruded itself, and which the fact that garments are regarded by the true native as a species of highly lacerated cuticle, was eminently calculated to overcome. However, a certain careless freedom, and withal a recklessness of mien, were not without explaining the present geographical position of the gentleman, and there was an easy adaptability in his genial face, quite in keeping with his surroundings. The faint scent of the wild verbena, mingled with the more brooding odor of buffalo-clover, steeped his senses as he quickened his horse's pace. Prairie-dogs, with the impudence of pigmies in their strongholds, barked at him as he passed, or suddenly disappeared in their burrows with a gurgling murmur of disapprobation at his invading progress. A crazy "killdee," screaming with the occasional aimlessness of an itinerant vender, ran before him upon the right, and with commendable counterfeiting of helplessness attempted to decoy him from her young. A jackass rabbit, plunging wildly from a neighboring bush, limped painfully away with its customary mendacity, and then turned and stared at him from under exaggerated ears. In emphatic derision of its hypocrisy, Howe put spurs to the intrepid "Oscar," compelling the shameless cripple to an exhibition of speed which disclosed its pitiful deception, and well nigh frightened into convulsions the would-be redoubtable "mule-ear."

After a prolonged and exhilarating canter

that drove the blood into the browned cheeks of the rider, he checked his horse with the perfumed breezes thrilling his pulses. As he did so, a lumbering gray owl of the horned species slipped from a neighboring live oak and flapped heavily away. Howe drew reign mechanically. Looking up into the near top of the dwarf tree from his elevated position, he espied a capacious nest in a secure fork, from which point of vantage two pairs of wondering eyes blinkingly regarded him. He immediately dismounted, tethered his horse by the lariat which hung from the pommel of his saddle, and proceeded to climb the tree. Arriving at the nest, he saw what he had before conjectured—two juvenile owls, partly fledged, and regarding him, with grotesque wisdom, from the midst of surrounding débris—the bones of moles and prairie-dogs, of tender years, purveyed for their delectation by their solicitous parents. In that spirit of dissent from the proclivities of animate nature which had actuated him all the morning, Howe, after a few moments of amused inspection, selected the most promising specimen of owldom and deposited him in the capacious pocket of his ducking-cloth jacket.

Not an instant too soon, though ; for the above-mentioned solicitous sire and mother, returning in company at this critical moment, attempted to interpose a forcible but unavailing remonstrance, as the triumphant thief slipped down the tree.

" Say—Mister—wot—ye—got ?" panted a mischievous voice behind him.

I mention it with regret, but candor compels it, that Mr. Howe gave a very violent start.

If there are any circumstances under which one is justified in deeming himself secure from the fair, it would seem that such might be realized upon the bald prairies of the South-west : and yet, anomalous as it may appear, encounters with a proverbially curious sex are not absolutely unknown. The vastness of the surroundings, the loneliness of the solitudes impart a feeling of isolation from feminine fascinations —a security against observation, so that the first impulse of surprise suggests an attack or at best an intrusion. He faced abruptly around. Seeing his evident amazement, his interrogator gave vent to a long, loud, extravagant but not unmusical explosion of laughter, accented by hilarious gestures of delight.

Howe entered upon a critical survey. The object of his scrutiny might be fairly said to challenge feminine classification. What he saw was a small figure so phenomenally clad in garments of either sex, that indecision as to gender was pardonable, to say the least. She had evidently been running, and her present merriment was heightened by the fact that she was quite out of breath. Her feet and ankles were bare, and somewhat scratched with the cat-claw and cactus, but—they were very small feet and ankles for all that. She wore a dress exhibiting similar signs of suffering from thorns, and through a diversity of three-cornered rents disclosing a red petticoat. Her hands did not appear, but a heavy hunting jacket, buttoned negligently about delicate little shoulders, and with several inches of superfluous sleeve, op-pressed rather than clad two slender arms, in-creasing the general air of incongruity and dis-comfort. A broad sombrero of felt, heavily adorned with tarnished silver lace and addi-tionally encumbered by a strap-band with double thong and buckles—conveying the impression of some primitive variety of cranial torture—formed her decidedly cumbrous head gear.

And yet the face that appertained to this much be-clothed picture of health was quaint and pretty. A pair of very roguish black eyes were discreetly presided over by long, fringing lashes. A braid of black hair, loosened by her recent activity, struggled from beneath her hat and fell upon her shoulder. The observant eye of Mr. Faye Howe detected a revolver worn rather ambitiously beneath the coat. With almost a sigh for a fastidious taste, fostered in feminine matters by past promenade concerts, he decided that she was about sixteen and unquestionably a very pretty young woman.

She suddenly regained her composure and spoke with damaging abruptness.

"Don't ye reckon yer 'shamed o' yerself —robbin' birds'-nests?" she asked boldly.

Somewhere in the depths of Howe's slumbering conscience there lurked a faint sense of shame for his present predicament. He tacitly acquiesced.

"Why did ye go to do it, then?" she inquired with the air of a privileged mentor.

"To give to you," he replied with a conciliating smile, finding his tongue at once in the fabrication of this entertaining falsehood,

This put a new construction on the case which the girl was quick to perceive. Gallantry, of however doubtful a character, is always appreciated by the artful sex. She was appeased but not convinced.

Dropping her chin suddenly, she exhibited to the gentleman's view a blank desert of hat, and appeared to commune with a precocious judgment beneath it. Finally raising her face again, and releasing her questioning eyes from their discreet, mourning fringes, "Will ye—will ye *swear* ye saw me?" she demanded with ridiculously solemn emphasis.

Mr. Howe was not at all positive that the circumstances demanded the gravity of an oath. He betrayed the weakness of his former position by an apparent reluctance to commit perjury.

"Reckon not!" she decided. "But will ye jest naturally give it to me—anyhow?" disclosing an entreating circle of pearl that was not to be resisted.

Something in the swooning fringes of those weeping lashes, the dewy freshness of the red lips, suggested to the young man the idea of compensation. I say *suggested* it. The gentleman had at one time been a law-student; he

had then been, for the time being, inclined to
doubt the material existence of compensation.
However, he still recognized it ideally. I submit, too, that it seemed really an age since he
had enjoyed the osculatory privileges of female
society. Actuated by a realizing sense of
this fact he made bold to declare his fell
design.

" I do not mind bestowing it upon one condition."

" How ? "

He started.   His ear was so sensitive to the
sound of his own name.

" Well ? "—with some mischief.

" What did ye jest get to say ? "

" I said you could have the owl on one con-
sideration."

" Wot's thet ? "

" A kiss,"—very grimly, as if inviting her to
a law-suit.

The girl retreated with feminine shyness ; her
hands, with difficulty asserting themselves from
the long sleeves, made haste to cover her presumably coveted mouth, as if in anticipation of
more practical advances. " No! thank ye ! "
she replied with awkward politeness. " I don't

go much on makin' free with perfect strangers.
Ye may keep yer ornery owl," she added.

Howe had just reached the same conclusion ;
he was provokingly ironical in reference to her
second sentence. Howbeit, he experienced that
enchantment which distance is said to lend to
unattainable objects.

Notwithstanding her recent disparaging comment, the girl still regarded the owl with inconsistent longing.

Howe confined his attention to a perusal
of her rustic attractions.

"Who are ye and where ye goin'?" she
finally demanded with charming directness.

"My name's Howe, and I'm on the road,"
he replied vaguely, exhibiting that Northern
privacy in personal matters unsympathized
with by the Southern temperament.

"Hope ye'll git thar ;" she responded cheerfully.

The gentleman thanked her for her good
wishes with an amused sarcasm, which was lost,
however, on its recipient.

"Wot's the name o' yer pony?" she said,
returning to the charge.

It happened that Mr. Faye Howe was trem-

bling on the verge of a sneeze. He was aware
of the Greek augury. He thought he would
sacrifice his politeness as a gallant to his classic
superstition. Besides, he was in Texas. If his
border-life had inculcated in the gentleman a
certain discretion which made him exclusively
addicted to indulging his forcible rhetoric in
the privacy of his own company, its influence
upon his code of social etiquette was apparently not so salutary. He permitted himself the
rude privilege, and did not find it necessary to
apologize, but he attempted to say "Oscar" at
the same moment.

"Hoss-car!" she exclaimed with scorn.
"'Pears to me ye ain't naturally got much taste.
Why didn't ye call him 'Sittin' Bull' or
'Standin' Buf'lo'? 'Pears to me men ain't
worth the flippin' a pecan a-namin' things.
There's Rube Smart's got two lovely mustangs,
he calls 'Snipe' and 'Bunch,' as ef he reckoned
one was a bird, and t'other a boil."

The girl regarded him with unqualified
contempt and seemed surprised that he did
not wither beneath it, but remarked very
calmly,

"I presume you would have called my horse

'Pansy' or 'Daisy'"—this, in malicious irony
of feminine christening.

An imperfect education in the repartee of the
border was not without assisting her in braving
the deductions of Mr. Howe's logic. She eyed
the mustang coolly and critically with the air
of a haughty connoisseur. I must admit with
grief for his æsthetic title, that his coat was
somewhat sun-cured and weather-beaten, and,
moreover, quite guiltless of grooming.

"No!" she said, "pardner, I skursely
reckon' I cud. 'Pears as I'd call him 'Quid'
or 'Terbacker.'"

Faye Howe lost his gravity at this sally, and
the young lady's scorn thawed a trifle at the
recognized compliment to her humor.

"Tell ye wot I reckon I'll do," she finally
said.

"What?" with exaggerated expectancy.

"I'll play ye fer thet thar critter," indicating
the owl by a disparaging wave of the hand.

"What will you put up against it?" inquired
Howe with well feigned caution, though heartily
amused.

The girl hesitated, glanced again at the owl,
sighed, and immediately decided.

"My six-shooter," drawing the formidable weapon.

"Done!" with a violent air of business. "What shall it be?"

"Poker," she said with easy familiarity, producing a woe-begone pack of cards from the side pocket of her coat.

The owl and revolver were placed side by side subject to the dictum of chance. The cards were cut and dealt in grave silence. The girl's cheeks flushed and her eyes gleamed with excitement.

"Two cards," she said with gratifying perfunctoriness.

Mr. Howe expressed himself as satisfied with his hand.

She scowled.

"Two pair—aces up!" said Howe.

"Full hand!" she shouted, triumphantly appropriating the spoils.

The gentleman acquiesced with an extravagant sigh of regret. Then *he* took the initiative in questioning.

"I suppose you can handle this?" he said, taking up the revolver—an old-fashioned, muzzle-loading Colt's "six-shooter."

" Right smart !" she said without looking up ;
she had become absorbed in lavish caresses of
the recently acquired owl.

" Let me see you shoot,"—Howe requested,
handing it over.

The girl accepted the weapon mechanically,
and looked around for a mark. She espied an
empty tomato-can, probably discarded by some
traveling teamster. She pointed it out to
Howe.

"Watch !" she quietly remarked, raising the
heavy weapon calculatingly in both her small
hands. Howe did watch with amused interest.

The startling report of the heavy arm followed, and as the smoke drifted to one side, the
can was seen to have changed its position with
visible damage.

Mr. Faye Howe was correspondingly awed
and appreciative.

" Bravo ! Where did *you* learn to shoot !" he
exclaimed approvingly.

" Oh ! Pop and me practices reg'lar 'bout the
ranch."

" The ranch ? Where's that ? "

" 'Bout a mile north o' here," she replied,

indicating the line by jerking the thumb of her right hand over **her** shoulder, while she still caressed **her** lugubrious **pet with** her left.

"Who lives there?"

"Me and Pop."

"Who's '*me*'?"

"Do **you** mean—what's my name?"

Howe nodded.

"Penelope Natchez," she answered.

"**What** does your father do?"

"What—does—he—do?" with round, amazed eyes. "Where ye bin, stranger? **Guess you're a** 'tender-foot.'"

"We're in equal 'fix,' sweetness," responded the collegian, apostrophizing **the little** bare and thorn-scratched feet.

The girl looked **at him** embarrassedly, **and** said **in an** instant, "Thet's plum a-plenty o' thet."

Mr. Howe made a mental note to avoid **comparisons** in the future.

"**Well,**" she resumed, after a silence, evidently protracted **for its** effect **as a moral** lesson, "if you're **so powerful** ignorant, my Pop is land-agent and sheep-raiser for Concho Co."

The gentleman reflected that **she probably**

shared the peculiarities of a charming but in-
accurate sex in matters of business. Concho Co.
being as large as the State of Rhode Island, it
was extremely unlikely that " Pop " monopolized
the sheep-industry for that extent of territory.
Howbeit, he looked wise and said nothing.

" Thar's part of 'em," she explained, pointing
out a small flock at a distance of several
hundred yards. . At times during the recent
conversation, Howe had fancied he heard the
bleating of sheep and lambs, but the sounds had
come so faintly against the wind that he believed
himself mistaken.

"Yer see," she said, drawing nearer to him
and becoming suddenly confidential, " Pop's
went down to Eden this morning to a trial;
he's a lawyer and has been county-judge—sure
'nuff. Bill Darcy's comin' up for shootin' a
feller, an' they couldn't get 'long no how without Pop. I promised him I'd herd them sheep
while he's away, because our herder's left. It's
somethin' I don't generally do," she concluded
apologetically.

This lucid explanation was not without interest to Howe. It happened that he was in
quest of this very same Judge Natchez in ref-

erence to a disputed land-title.   In view of her
recent charming confidences, he briefly developed these facts to Miss Penelope.

"Reckon ye'd better stop at the ranch to-
night," she said, when he had finished. "Pop'll
be back by sun-down. Ye can lunch with me
under thet live oak, ef ye care to—over *yonder*,"
pointing to a tree rather larger in its general
outline than the prevailing type of that dwarf
caricature of an apple-tree.   It was distant
about a hundred yards.

"But my sheep's strayin'! *Throw 'em in,
Flo!*" she screamed to a black and white shepherd-dog that now disclosed herself in their
neighborhood, and had been doing double duty
in her mistress' absence.

"*Go—'round—'em!*" gesticulating with a cir-
cular wave of the hand.

The intelligent brute looked knowingly at
her a moment, and then trotting off, made a
wide *détour* to intercept the stragglers. But
there was now a commotion among the loudly
lamenting flock, and a disturbed bleating came
distinctly to the ear.

"Does thet 'Hoss-car' o' yours 'buck,' Mr.
Howe?" inquired Miss Penelope.

The gentleman felt a certain pride in disclaiming for his mustang that customary Texan characteristic.

"Reckon I'll hev to borrer him, then," she said, loosing the tethered pony, springing into the saddle, and throwing her knee over its Mexican pommel; "I'll meet ye over by thet tree." And she rode away like the wind with an Amazonian *abandon* quite in keeping with her general manner.

Bidden thus to an Arcadian repast and deprived of his horse, there was nothing for Faye Howe to do but to follow her instructions. He set out for the appointed rendezvous, but being possessed of some curiosity to note the precision of her recent shot, turned first in the direction of the unfortunate can. Doubtless, he proceeded with less than his customary caution, for he was immediately afterward startled violently by a peculiar warning, very similar to the rapid uncoiling of a broken clock-spring—a sound never forgotten by one who has heard it under dangerous circumstances. Bewildered by its muffled character, he sprang suddenly to one side, and stepped right upon an enormous rattle-snake. Almost identical in color with the "curly mesquite" grass in its neighborhood, it lay coiled ready to spring. He shrank back with an exclamation of horror but was too late. The reptile darted forward, with a movement of its head like successive, rapid blows of a tack-hammer. With a sickening shudder the gentleman felt himself bitten in the little finger of his right hand.

He staggered, ghastly pale, to the live oak— distant but a few yards—and fell, rather than sat down, beneath its shade. He was faint with agony. Cold beads of perspiration—like a death damp—started upon his forehead. A foot-fall struck his ear; he raised his head in a blind, dazed fashion. The girl was already returning, holding the owl.

"Wot's up?" she queried, her quick eyes noting the feebleness of his attitude.

"Bitten!" he gasped, trying to smile in the presence of the *weaker* sex—presumably. It was a ghastly failure—that smile.

The girl became a heroine with Columbine suddenness. The owl, projected from his airy perch, described a bewildered parabola. She was kneeling beside him.

"Quick! strip up yer shirt sleeve!" she

cried, tearing the band from her heavy hat. She wrapped the leathern thong about his muscular fore-arm, and slipping the straps in the buckles, applied this rude tourniquet with an excited, nervous strength that made him wince. She produced a small pistol-flask and some matches. "Show me!" she said imperatively.

Mr. Faye Howe *obeyed*. His little finger, his wrist—his whole hand and fore-arm, up to the leathern bandage, were so swollen they might have done justice to Goliath of Gath.

Dropping to a sitting posture, she deposited her sombrero in her lap, and grasping his wrist firmly, she laid the hand upon the thick felt.

Have you ever seen a woman fumble and flounder with a powder flask? This Texan heroine deposited two charges upon the bite, as deftly as she handled her needle when she cared to. She struck a lucifer. Howe gave a gesture of disapproval.

"Grit yer teeth!" she said coolly. She dropped the match. A flash; a sizzling sputter; a puff of white smoke. Mr. Faye Howe yelled of course.

"Thar!" she said, with a sigh of relief, "I reckon that'll naturally fetch it."

After which exhibition of decision, feminine nerves betrayed themselves; she trembled violently and looked a little faint. However, she was spared the observance of this by her companion. He began to be taken with a convulsive shuddering. Summoning her courage again, the girl began to pull and tug at the pocket of her coat. She finally extricated a reluctant, colossal, flat bottle. It was despondently full. She uncorked it.

"Drink!" she said simply. "Scotch whisky! yer *life* depends on it!"

Howe took a long pull at the flask.

"Don't stop!" she cried. "There's heaps more! I've got it hid at the ranch. Lucky I kep' this from Pop last night," she soliloquized. "I was afeard he was 'lowin to get outside of this, so as to clear Darcy. It's most too pop'lar with Pop. Reckon by this time," she added confidentially, as if to her bare feet, "ther' wouldn't been nothin' in it but the smell, if he'd been bit. 'Pears he's been bit reg'lar every evenin' lately." Then she turned to Howe and said sternly, "Why don't ye *drink ?*"

Thus adjured, Howe made a laudable effort

to diminish the contents of the flask. Penelope watched him anxiously.

"Yer must drink it all," she protested, "and
then—" looking at him slyly, as if to note the
impression made by her bibulous advice—"and
then—yer must begin on the dimmy-john.
Stop ter take breath; throw yer head back;
shut yer eyes, and let her june; the objek is
ter get the pizen drunk." After which graphic
medical treatise, she subsided with a solicitous
gravity in her eloquent black eyes.

The contents of the flask were seriously
diminishing. Howe felt no exaltation from the
liquor. It was the antagonism of the virus.

"Ye must get home," Penelope suddenly
said in anxiety.

"Home?" said Howe, wanderingly.

"Yes—to the ranch."

She picked up the unfortunate owl, which,
from its apparent distress, had not even yet
regained its wonted equanimity.

"Come," she said, shaking the lethargic gentleman, "tumble into yer saddle while there's
time."

He mechanically obeyed her. She called to
her dog to "throw her sheep together." Tak-

ing the **lariat of the** impassive **"Oscar,"** who
had been **an apparently** æsthetic and stupid
spectator **of her** previous efforts **for** his unfortunate **master, she drove the** bleating flock
before her and set out for the ranch.

III.

THE nest-building of the Texan **is not char-**
acterized by that air of luxurious **refine-**
ment which **once obtained** among **older**
Southern states. **The humble dwelling of the**
ex-judge, land-agent, **and sheep-farmer, I** regret
to say, **was not an exception.** Notwithstanding
that wealth **of ability which his** varied pursuits
might seem to imply, mechanical art interposed
but an obscure and feeble shield between **him
and the** inclemency of the weather. **This may
have been** owing to a stoical **indifference to
climatic changes,** but **I am inclined to refer it
to a certain carelessness, and implicit faith in
nature, quite in keeping** with the Texan temperament. **The idea of** *carelessness* was strength-
ened **in the** mind **of** the casual visitor **by**
marked shiftlessness in material surroundings,

and by apparently impotent efforts to discard
articles of departed utility. The surface of the
bald prairie, which undulated like a beach of
sand upon the borders of the ranch, exhibited
the same disreputable curiosities that are sometimes found on the shore of the sea. Tin cans,
empty bottles, soleless boots, broken crockery,
hats, shameless in their battered exterior—
all in absurd attitudes of vagrancy—covered
the desecrated face of virgin solitude. The
forlorn emblems of ephemeral adornment were
all persistently and uninterestingly masculine.
It is with embarrassment that I admit, that
there were other articles, unmistakably feminine.

·Among a heap of deer-horns, bleached and
weather-crumbling, an object gaunt and destitute of grace intruded itself. Lying thus amid
the débris of ambitious, natural head-gear, its
vertebrate outline might have been taken for
the wasted skeleton of the animal to which the
smaller antlers once belonged, but a more critical eye declared it to be unquestionably—a
discarded "*long-bustle*." Familiar and privileged intimacy with the feminine details of
ranches makes me conscious of an unfortunate

ability to dilate upon still more intricate developments of the gentler sex, but I forbear. Suffice it to say, that such articles as were thus gratuitously and generously offered to examination, were explored and appreciated by sundry wild-cattle. In the inquiring search of the salt-starved prairie-kine, these unlaundried waifs received minute dental and even masticatory attention.

The ranch itself had been rather injudiciously built at the junction of two creeks, and on a very slight knoll in a small encircling clump of live oaks—their ever-green quality offering thus a feeble but perennial shade. It was of *adobe* and undoubtedly picturesque. Its capacity for comfort at certain seasons was apparently beneath the attention of its owner. The roof from within afforded occasional astronomical opportunities, and a pane of glass in the solitary window was rendered uselessly opaque by the intervention of an old felt hat. Howbeit, it was not altogether unprepossessing.

It had once been the apartment of the accomplished Judge, but as the flight of time marked a growing maturity in Penelope, the legal gentleman had exhibited a chivalric

courtesy in retiring to the less pretentious, but
equally leaky, cover of a tent, pitched just outside. This, with enforced retreats at odd
times to the kitchen—a long, low structure,
built of slabs and graced with a small cooking-
stove—formed the father's sleeping quarters,
and comprised his somewhat sad attempt at
house-keeping. The whole was encircled by a
slight rail-fence.

The chivalric retirement of the Judge from
Miss Penelope's room, was, however, tempered
by signs of his intermittent presence. A
meager array of the resources of Texan jurisprudence in the shape of three debilitated law-
books, covered with dust, and secured from
perusal by over-topping feminine "gimcracks,"
was supplemented by an ample commentary
sanctioned by one Lynch J.—to whom frontier
ideas of exact justice apparently necessitated
more assiduous reference. Briefly, the wall in
the neighborhood of the scant law-library suggested an arsenal. It was literally frescoed
with munitions of war—shot-guns, "Winchesters," carbines, pistols, revolvers, and bowies,
were included in this suggestive display of the
swift retribution that waits upon crime. It is

not too much to say, that, with the exception of
several articles of apparel, discreetly veiled by
an overhanging strip of calico, they formed
almost the only details of this modest attempt
at house-furnishing.   There was, however, one
other prominent piece of furniture.   A low
bed, somewhat shaky in its underpinning, and
exhibiting that peculiar sketchiness in make-up
of which the interior, and, in fact, the *tout
ensemble* of this caricature of mechanical art
prevailingly partook.

Mr. Faye Howe was, at present, occupying
it. A demi-john rested upon the floor.   Penelope, tin cup in hand, with a grim resolve in
her pretty features and a general atmosphere
of perfunctory dosing, was seated near him.   It
is only the grave exigency of his recent misfortune which constrains me to admit that the
gentleman was, at present, hopelessly inebriated.
At the interesting moment of his introduction
the laudable and unremitting attentions of
Miss Natchez had accomplished this unfortunate but necessary result.

Yet, whether it is to be attributed to the
potency of the poison or to his naturally strong
head, I somehow feel it necessary to say, by

way of apology, that he had not succumbed without a struggle.

Had Penelope been interested in drunkenness as a purely psychical study, it is to be believed that, at successive stages, her experimental efforts would have been amply rewarded. But she was eminently practical, and ignored details. Serene in the achievement of her purpose, attendant symptoms were disregarded. The phenomena attributable to alcoholic excess are almost infinite. The ardent devotion of some temperaments when intoxicated is worthy of a higher inspiration. I think I am safe in saying that, whatever possibilities liquor may induce, Mr. Howe achieved them all. He had been hilarious, maudlin, affectionate, even endearing. He was now feebly interjectional and mildly incoherent. His naturally retentive memory, excited by his potions, constrained him at first to entertain Miss Natchez with a lengthy rehearsal of acknowledged vocal abilities. He sang solos, duets, trios—his intoxicated judgment even tempting him to grapple with a quartet. This proving a lamentable failure—especially as he evinced a disposition to carry all the parts at once—he relapsed into college-glees, **and eventually into** a madly **whirling** drinking-chorus.

Awakening **to a realizing** sense of his proximity **to beauty, he** exhausted **the** resources of sentiment **and an** unusually rich vocabulary **upon the** astonished maiden. **He called** her "his flower," "his life," "his **dream,"** "his 'brooding sweetness,'" his "ecstatic **affinity."** He was evidently near **the** clouds **at** this point. He even instituted comparisons, **and** drawing from the bosom of his blowse the *carte-de-visite* of a most fashionably-dressed young **lady, expressed** his unhesita**ting preference for** the natural charms **of his** *bizarre* **nurse.** These **vehement efforts were associated with** certain familiarities **of** gesture **and caress, which** Penelope **repelled with** commendable coyness, but **with a manifest** feebleness, prompted, no **doubt, by her** feminine consciousness of **the** fact **that his** critical discernment was **sadly** blunted **by the** frequency of his libations. **In** the end, worn out by **his violent exertions, Mr.** Faye Howe became helplessly **comatose. Miss** Penelope Natchez **picked** up the picture that had fallen from **his** nerveless fingers. She abandoned herself **to a** long and careful **study** of its attractions. Having concluded which, with the disparaging comment that she "didn't go much on sich fine-haired and furbelowed gals as thet," she heaved a deep sigh, and with a tender glance at the recumbent Howe, ruthlessly appropriated it.

It was now night. "Pop" had not come home. With some forebodings for her sire's present physical condition, she essayed to allay her filial anxiety by renewed efforts for the comfort of Howe. Now that he was entirely unconscious, she lavished a wealth of tenderness upon him; she lifted his head and deposited it in her lap; she passed her hands caressingly over the blonde beard, and softly smoothed his thin hair; she talked to him cooingly, in a sympathetic, pitying fashion, deprecating his misfortune, and sincerely grateful for her prompt presence. And then, as time slipped away into the small hours, and the moonlight—that mysterious foe of woman—filtered through the well-ventilated roof and fell upon her; and the mocking-birds—those melodious extollers of Luna's demoralizing tendencies—beguiled her with their song, she grew suddenly lonely; her head drooped, her black

mane touched his **forehead**, and **she** *kissed* him.
And the half-fledged **but vigilant owlet**, as if by
this seal **he recognized her** now inalienable title
to his **chance-ownership**, attested **it by a** soft
" Hoo-o ! Hoo-o-o !" that **sent the** hot blood
dancing over the girl's temples, **as** though a
cloud of witnesses were conscious **of her** weak-
ness. But Mr. Faye Howe dreamed **that the**
fashionable lady watched over his **sleep.**

IV.

THE following morning, **as Judge** Natchez,
who comprehended **under** one large hat-brim
so much of the professional ability of Concho
County, turned his face homeward, **there was**
an air of dejection about his bearing, and a
flavor of delinquency in the swift canter **into**
which **he at once** lashed his unambitious **pony.**
It is very likely that this gloomy **exterior was**
the outcome **of** certain **reverses,** professional
and pecuniary, that the gentleman **had** recently
sustained. **N**otwithstanding copious draughts
of that inspiration, **which,** according to Miss
Natchez, " Pop " was wont to imbibe, his earn-

est eloquence in behalf of his client was unap-
preciated, and Bill Darcy had been sentenced
to be hung. And the legal gentleman's efforts
to drown his chagrin in the enticements of
" Mexican Monte," during the previous evening, or more precisely, to "even up with the
Almighty," as he profanely remarked, on sitting
down to the deal board, had unfortunately resulted in the loss of his retainer and counsel-
fee, consisting of the sum of twenty-five dollars *cash* and a diamond pin—his client's title
to this last article being entirely limited to
the ostentatious wearing of the gem.

There was a pathetic terseness in his summary of his woes to the proprietor of the Eden
Saloon.

" Busted, Jim, mental, moral and physical.
' Hang me up ' for better luck, and recooperate
my failin' powers with a ' stone-fence '."

It was apparently impossible for human nature
to resist this appeal. The drink was speedily
placed before him by the gentlemanly proprietor, who mixed it himself in the easy freedom
of shirt-sleeves and tilted cigar.

Having deposited this ominous beverage in
his stomach with the air of one assuming the

carriage of unusually heavy freight, Natchez
departed. Howbeit, it was the second section
of stone-wall which he had that morning assim-
ilated. He mixed the other himself, and meas-
ured the whisky on the "two-finger" princi-
ple—having lost the middle and third digit
down at San Antonio in a little difference of
opinion between a legal scholar and himself
about the law of *mayhem.* This slight mutila-
tion, however, he was unwilling should destroy
the consistency of his original method.

I may remark parenthetically at this point,
that the gentlemanly proprietor of the Eden
Saloon, as aggregating in his collective indi-
viduality the functions of hotel-proprietor,
bar-keeper, and gambler, typified in the mind
of Penelope the Serpent of Biblical Story, with
the general outlines of whose disreputable
advice to confiding womanhood and subsequent
depressing influence upon mankind in general,
she was mistily familiar. The gentleman was
accordingly despised with the customary inten-
sity of a discriminating sex when reprehensible
qualities are unquestionably labeled. So that,
one would have imagined *primâ facie* a seem-
ing inconsistency in the despondency with

which the legal Adam dashed through the narrow street of this frontier travesty of Paradise.

An hour later he chanced upon a black-browed Hercules, lying listlessly upon the prairie, and gazing with a scowl at some very fine cattle grazing in a fertile hollow. The man was attired in the unmistakable clothes of his calling. There were the heavy, wide, leathern leggings extending to the waist, giving the wearer, when erect, the appearance of walking in an immense mail-bag. There were the knee-boots with heels so extravagantly high, and placed at such an absurd angle, that a *Parisienne* in the day of *Louis Quinze* would have screamed with delight and cheerfully acquiesced in so admirable a contrivance for destroying the eyesight. This gentleman avoided any such tendency by living in the saddle. When he decided to walk—which he rarely did—he strongly personified in gait that inelegant bird —the goose. It was the American cow-boy, *par excellence*, with a certain smartness of exterior, which suggested the approving criticism of the fair.

A small tent stood near him, sharing by its general air of relaxation in the despondency

which seemed rampant that morning. **The
necessary conveniences** and utensils of his **tent**
were strewn **in reckless** and crippled confusion
about their **recumbent** owner. This ill-favored
nomad seemed **to be** lying amid rheumatic and
despondent household **gods.**

What was there in the **sight of** those mag-
nificent cattle to occasion **that scowl?** It **was
simply a question of** " cow-brands." **He** was
in despair **of any** possible method by **which**
that " wine-glass **" label** could be converted **with**
the assistance **of a red-hot iron into his own**
suspiciously involved **trade-mark. This is Mr.
R**ube Smart—" cow-puncher."

Intuitively recognizing a sympathetic spirit,
the Judge checked **his** horse.

" **H-h-howdy!" the "** stone-fence **"** rather
than the Judge remarked. The man, recogniz-
ing the bibulousness of his salute, **raised
his eyes in** surly inquiry **and replied,**
" Howdy!"

" Bo-oo-'ful **mornin'!"**

The man **shrugged his shoulders** and ungra-
ciously accepted **the** weather's serenity. The
peculiarly **rocky character** of the Judge's cups
had not communicated their insensibility to his

perceptions. He was conscious of a lack of spontaneity in the dialogue.

"Wash up? Wash lates' newsh fro' Washington?" he queried with judicial concern, and, I grieve to say, with occasional Texan-judicial articulation.

"Bill Darcy's sentenced ter swing," said the cow-boy. The peculiar quality of ironical exaggeration by which the Judge's inadequate defense was rendered a national matter, was keenly felt by its recipient through his spirituous disguise. His effusiveness was quenched.

"Wash feller 'shpec' 'shgot five mur'hers an' dead nigger 'ghin 'm," he retorted.

"Judge," said his gloomy auditor with affected concern, "I reckon you'd better pull yer freight fer hum; this sun's a heap too hot fer yer head, and I don't reckon ther's room enough roun' here fer ye. I'd recommen' yer ter put right smart o' water on that law-box o' your'n when yer git thar. What's more," he continued, "thet Penelope"—he alluded to Miss Natchez as though she suggested *antelope*, with the attributes of which he was unquestionably more familiar—"thet Penelope o' your'n needs yer protectin' care. I seen her, yesterday, totin' a fine-haired feller up to yer ranch. Looked kinder caved in, blank him!" he concluded, with a lowering look. The Judge did not inquire into the origin of his friend's profanity. He was oppressed with graver personal misgivings.

"I reckon thar's whar my whisky's been junein'!" Apparently sobered by the gravity of this decision he wheeled his horse, and rode off without thanking his informant.

V.

WHEN Mr. Faye Howe first opened his blood-shot blue eyes on the morning after his sanitary debauch, a demoralized sensation of dull pain oppressed his bewildered consciousness. His digestive apparatus seemed to have experienced abnormal distention and subsequent disastrous collapse. His head was the only bodily organ which appeared to be still subject to inflation, and his mouth and throat—he was morally convinced, had usurped the functions of the descent to Avernus. He lay perfectly still, overwhelmed with the idea

that the present colossal proportions of his
cranium required all the space of Penelope's
airy boudoir for their accommodation, and that
the slightest change of position would release
a throbbing engine in his skull, and involve its
very sensitive walls in crushing ruin. By what
species of inspiration he had engineered his
gigantic head-piece through the narrow doorway was a problem beyond the present available resources of his whisky-steeped intellect.
He was still feebly pondering upon the impossibilities of this achievement, when Penelope
dawned upon him through the portal, so
ambitiously transformed from the Bohemian
toilet of yesterday, that failure of recognition
by him, in his present shattered condition,
might have been pardonable. She was con-
sistently feminine in her attire, but extravagantly arrayed in finery of a faded and filmy
texture. Nevertheless, a certain witchery
about the *tout ensemble*, and an agreeable odor
of buffalo-clover with which her hair and antiquated corsage were adorned, made its impression upon Howe, who yielded her the homage
of a sex more appreciative of effect than detail
in matters of dress. He was not without

glimpses of the damsel's possibilities in appropriate attire.

"Howdy?" she said, in a sprightly tone. "How ye makin' out?" with a sympathy of manner which her grammar would scarcely convey.

Howe thanked her, and exhibited a diffidence about expatiating upon his sensations, feeling a man's incapacity to do the subject complete justice without the assistance of profane rhetoric. He ventured, however, to photograph his hygienic degradation by facial pantomime.

"Prezackly!" she exclaimed with demure eyelashes, but mentally charmed by the contrast between his silence and her sire's unhallowed inspirations after indiscreet libations to Silenus. She displayed at once a savory bowl and large spoon, which she had hitherto held behind her.

"I reckoned ye'd be just naturally starved arter yesterday," she said, "so I jes' killed a pullet and made ye some chicken broth. Yer hand's better, Mr. Howe. Tell ye, honey, ye had a clus call—sure 'nuff."

Forthwith a prairie Hebe began to minister to the famished capacity of a blonde Bacchus.

Meanwhile, her respected parent, having struck a most uncompromising, homeward bee-line since his last cheerful information, was just rising the divide which overlooked his ranch. As he crossed the string of water-holes which formed the line of the creek, he was instantly cognizant of the fact, that although the qualifications of the day for pasturage were admirable, his sheep were still imprisoned in their primitive brush-pen, and were solacing their appetites on the haystack which he had prudently provided against the advent of dreaded "Northers." This being the last link in the chain of misfortunes which had lately oppressed him, he at once entered into hearty and blasphemous rivalry of the much-afflicted Job, who—I cheerfully submit—was fairly successful in exhausting the poetic possibilities of profanity.

It is with reluctance that I refrain from transcribing this Homeric indulgence in epithet. For I certainly appreciate how necessary it is to the interpretation of character, and to the por-

trayal of an exceptional felicity of expression.
I concede, however, for the reader's enlighten-
ment, that he threw grave and unsanctified
doubts on the origin of himself and Penelope,
and in a surprisingly short space of time
involved his entire genealogical line in unquestionable discredit, making all this contingent
upon certain conditions of which he had present
ocular proof.

After which charming effort he executed a
wild war-dance in his stirrups in evidence of an
exhausted vocabulary, took out a large, black
plug of tobacco and bit off a triangular quarter
of it, and then charged headlong upon his
abode.

It would, perhaps, be reasonable to presume
after the late explosion, and the additional
revelation of the recently absorbed virtues of
his demi-john and flat bottle — both of which
rested in odoriferous emptiness outside his hospitable door—that the Judge girded his loins to
do battle with the presumed whisky absorbent.
But he did not. The education of the Judge
must be remembered ; it was legal and rhetor-
ical, with that contempt for physical proficiency
which the cultivation of the intellect frequently

implies. In the exchange of professional
billingsgate or personal repartee, he excited
the admiration and applause of Concho Co.
This natural gift for fluent invective was, perhaps, assisted in no slight degree by the fact
that he was very deaf, and his feelings, being,
therefore, spared the damaging reflections of
his opponents, permitted his untrammeled intellect to rise calm and clear to every verbal
emergency. His peculiar mental attitude was
thus superior to the employment of brute
force, and when an array of adverse circumstances intruded themselves upon his normally
serene exterior, he was prone to invite Divine
attention to his wrongs in the irreverent manner
we have indicated. The Judge, by temperament, and Mr. Howe, by experience, were con-
sistent in this regard.

But on the present occasion, whatever verbal
collation he had reserved for Mr. Faye Howe,
he was apparently prevented from offering to
his notice, partly by his instant recognition
of his familiar features, and partly by that apparent interest in his daughter which he
detected in the gentleman's face as he entered
the room. He recognized in him a very good

client; he was aware of his plethoric bank-account. This was the first occasion on which the Northerner had honored his legal adviser by visiting him at his own abode; and the father's imaginative temperament and fond parental heart were at once inspired with air-castle tendencies for the possible future of Miss Penelope.

His greeting, therefore, although subdued in utterance, was earnest and genuine. The Judge prevailingly adopted a mildness of intonation in ordinary conversation; it was effective as expressive of his utter hopelessness of hearing his own voice.

I may as well acquaint the reader, at this point, with the fact that the gentleman was of unquestionable birth and breeding. He was the son of a former governor of the State of Virginia, and Penelope's mother had been a lady of patrician beauty and social attraction; but the War, that comprehensive apology for much Southern shamelessness of destitution, was here sincere. The feebler feminine nature despaired and died; the stronger masculine one survived and accepted alcoholic consolation. When, therefore, the degenerate gentleman of a once golden age learned of **the narrow** escape of his guest, and the heroic treatment extended by **his** daughter, his **pale,** intellectual, **and still hand-some** features **expressed** both parental pride **and** sympathetic **solicitude.**

Neither am **I prepared** to admit that the apparent dearth **of alcoholic** refreshment detracted **at** all from **his natural joy at** unmistakable symptoms of **convalescence. Let** those who doubt, experience **Southern hospitality.**

" Penelope will bring you **around in a day or two,"** he said cheerfully ; " **make yourself perfectly at home and as comfortable as you** can **under the circumstances. ˙Meanwhile,** you **say you** have certain **matters of business "**—the **critical** reader observes **that the J**udge had that easy adaptability **which enabled him to vary** his dialect **to suit his auditor, and his present** utterance gave evidence **of the recollection** of social privileges, once enjoyed and **by no means for-gotten—**" we can consider them at our leisure."

To which **Howe—a** Northerner, remember, and notwithstanding **his serious** invalidism, **replied :**

" **Why not now ? It's the old** matter—that **dispute about** water-privileges between Smart and myself. **The** season **is dry,** and **there is** barely enough **for my** six thousand sheep. **He** insists upon watering his cattle on my range."

"**Is** thet all **?**" said the legal gentleman, relapsing into border slang immediately, and giving fiery **advice** which, hitherto, **he** had seldom followed. "Is thet all? Wal, I've looked up **thet** matter an' **yer** 'files' is all straight ; give him 'notice to quit;' ef he dont 'bluff,' shove half a dozen cartridges inter yer 'Winchester,' freeze ter yer water-hole, and stand **off** him and his cussed cattle."

•

VI.

A FORTNIGHT of the halcyon weather of a Texan spring had passed away—days of sunshine, of fragrance, of bird-song—the blossoming of Nature's heart in earth, and air, and sky—days uneventful, but, ah me ! **full of a cer-** tain novel and blissful fascination **for Miss** Natchez. She was leaning dejectedly over the narrow railing **of** the ranch, **her** drooping eyelashes giving **her** face a quaint suggestion of **heavy** mourning. There had been no abate-

ment of the glad weather; the air was tremulous with the melody of rival mocking-birds
which flickered in black and white plumes from
tree to tree, and filled the embowering live
oaks with their delirious ventriloquism. Her
cause of grief was entirely subjective; the sunshine of Mr. Faye Howe's presence had faded
from her horizon.

There had been hours of Arcadian colloquy,
of equestrian companionship, of pastoral sheep-
tending and sheep-seeking with this Lone Star
Bo-peep. There had even been sentimental
moments of generous rivalry, devoted to the
perforation of tin tomato-cans at ten paces
with the "six-shooter." It would seem that
the "abomination of desolation" was left as
the result of this target-practice.

Howbeit, although at times given to reverie
and a day dreaming that was new to her, she
was full of a certain energy attributable, perhaps,
to the awakening spring. But the Judge, who
was himself a victim of the "dumb-ager," and,
on days consecrated to mental communion and
suppressed "shakes," had an invalid's acute
perceptions, "allowed thet he never reckoned
the 'spring fever' so obstrep'rous."

A sudden conviction of the untidiness of the ranch oppressed her, and by incessant practice in the hurling of missiles, she removed its encircling débris to a point too remote for ocular disapprobation.

Then she lost her apparent taste for veiling her sex in masculine raiment. With the aid of some old fashion-plates, and an ingenuity with her needle at which the sterner sex stands aghast, she accomplished *toilettes outré* but effective, from relics of her mother's finery religiously preserved by her father. The Judge had his failings; he had also his ideals. Notwithstanding great powers of fascination for a proverbially confiding sex, he never found it in his heart, nor in his wildest dreams believed it possible, to duplicate Mrs. Natchez.

Her dress-making over, Penelope developed marvels of cleanliness, and entered upon a campaign against her luxuriant but tangled mane. She possessed among her treasures a cracked and bilious mirror. Before this mendacious detractor she passed unlimited time in the industrious combing and effective arrangement of her raven tresses. It is interesting, as an instance of the intuition of woman, that she

merely pursued the man-demoralizing tactics
of the famous "Lorelei," of whose entirely
poetic existence she was blissfully in ignorance.

Finally, having carefully prepared the sinews
of feminine warfare in the formal manner above
described, she drew the picture of the unfortunately fashionable young lady from the
humiliation of the chimney, affixed it to a
tree with a small "bowie," and being geo-
graphically prevented from annihilation of the
lady by pure personal charm, engaged in vin-
dictive and unerring target-practice upon it
with a more effective but no more remorseless
weapon.

But I think it was in her treatment of the
owl that she most palpably acknowledged the
presence of Cupid. She possessed a small
menagerie of native pets with which her hitherto undeveloped affections had been content.
In small wooden cages she had immured at various stages of adolescence, a dove, a mocking-
bird, a prairie-dog, a diminutive jackass-rabbit.
A somewhat lively fancy in the detection
of resemblances had impelled her to baptize
these captives with the titles of certain of her

many admiring suitors. She shared the Homeric fascinations of the model wife of Ulysses. The dove and the mocking-bird were cow-men of mild and languishing sentimentality in feminine matters—Nature's carpet-knights—the one given to playing cooing ballads on horse-back with a cracked guitar, and the other offensive through a servile semblance of devotion, at spasmodic intervals, on a reedy accordion. The marmot was Mr. James Wily—the gambler ; the jack-rabbit was Mr. Rube Smart—the " cow-puncher."

But the owl,—the owl! was nameless, typical of that evasive silence which woman preserves in amatory matters of a serious complexion. Howbeit, the desperate devotion with which she sacrificed before this silent, feathered altar might have encouraged the ancient Pythagoras in his doctrine of metempsychosis.

She decorated him with ribbons and garlands ; she ignored his indifference ; she quailed before the staring scrutiny of those great eyes, as if she believed that behind them lurked the remembrance of her osculatory weakness. Penelope had hitherto enjoyed the reputation of uniform tenderness toward dumb animals, but, in her efforts to satisfy the exorbitant appetite of Minerva's bird, she traversed many miles and stained her immaculate record with the blood of slaughtered innocents. In the unself-ish inthrallment of her absorbing passion, I am even fearful that a dearth of provision might have turned her predatory intentions to her former pets. The teeming life of the wilds spared her this additional guilt, but the ignored four suffered the diet of departed fascination.

One morning an accommodating teamster jumped down from his box-seat in his " prairie-schooner," and deposited in her trembling fin-gers a *billet-doux ;* she devoured its contents with eager eyes. It was simply an invitation to a ball to take place that evening at Eden, but it was from Howe, and its effect was alarm-ing.

She became earnestly grave and set about appalling formalities ; she filled the clothes-boiler of the ranch and heated it to a danger-ous temperature ; she removed all the interior furnishings of her father's tent, tightened its cords, and rendered it nearly opaque ; she de-posited within it her most elaborate *toilette* and an ambitious wash-tub. Then taking her " six-shooter," she chastely retreated within its precincts, and tied down the canvas opening from within. This modern Diana recognized the efficiency of powder and ball against a possible Actæon. When she reappeared the effect was dazzling in the extreme.

That the ball was held in a vacant store owned by Jim Wily; that it was illuminated by an unpardonable extravagance in tallow-dips, perched upon laths tacked to empty shelves; that the *élite* of Eden danced in full equipment but in the affluence of "boiled shirts"; and that the social sub-stratum, from every available window and loop-hole, availed themselves of a view of the festivities in which they were not invited to participate, but which they endeavored to cloud by the diabolical tobacco-smoke under which they veiled their slighted feelings, is a matter of memory among the inhabitants of the frontier town. But how Miss Penelope Natchez was its pervading charm, how she outshone by her bewildering appearance the much be-toileted fair; how she compelled admiration by flatly refusing to dance with Jim Wily, while not hesitating to grace his entertainment with the effulgence of her presence; how she danced square dances with all her many admirers, but how there was a tendency to monotony in waltzing with Mr. Faye Howe, was reported at great length by the ornate editor of the Eden Advertiser, whose extravagant periods afforded significant evidence of the height to which a single privileged quadrille had exalted him. We have lost our copy of this gifted sheet or we could not forbear transcribing. But while Penelope and Faye were approximating to a condition of plastic infatuation at this crowning social event of the frontier season, there were two who departed with far different feelings : Mr. Jim Wily in expressive indignation ; and Mr. Rube Smart in the embrace of the "green-eyed monster."

VII.

AN exceptionally hot and dry summer brought with it a train of disasters to the stock-men of Concho Co. The pitiless heavens denied rain ; the baked plain was opulent with crumbling dust ; the water in the stagnant pools evaporated to mere dimples of silver in the starved cheeks of the brown prairie. The

grass withered **and died** before **the hot** breath
of the sirocco.   **An** acrid smoke by day which
smarted **the** eyes, **and an** ominous glow in the
heavens at night, were Nature's telegrams of a
more fearful destroyer—the prairie fire.   It
was **a** season of great discouragement and ter-
rible loss, and the tempers and deeds of men
harmonized perfectly with their material surroundings.

The relations of Mr. Howe and Mr. Smart
were necessarily belligerent.   The former's apparent progress in the affections of Miss Natchez
effectually settled **that.**   Throughout the long,
dry season **Rube's stock** drank **the** water of
the Northern gentleman's **" range "** by **the**
hogshead : at first, under **his** armed surveil-
lance ; afterward, with the familiar effrontery **of**
habit.   At last, when a further continuance of
this would have left his own woolly flocks to
famish, Howe laid aside his customary caution,
filled the magazine of his " Winchester," and
getting the " first drop " upon his persistent
foe, coolly assured him **of** speedy conversion
into a human colander, **if** he did not desist *in-*
stanter.   There was a steely glitter in Howe's
usually mild blue eye, aside from **the** advan-

tage of his attitude, which was convincing. Mr. Rube Smart accepted the resistlessness of the gentleman's logic. He quietly withdrew.

This did not prevent him, however, from emptying his own carbine and " six-shooter " on occasional dark nights into the crowded sheep-pens of the Northerner. The dastardly cowardice of this act was apparently visited with retribution, for Rube's stock—few in number and mostly acquired by conversion, both literal and legal—died by tens and scores. His encounter with the Northerner had sufficiently convinced him that open combat was not the most efficient method for revenge.

Assisted by Jim Wily, who still rankled, and by Texan rum of phenomenally bad quality, he developed a scheme, worthy of the brain from which it emanated and the liquor by which it was inspired. Briefly, his plan was to "pop the question " to Miss Penelope, and in the event of her probable refusal, to pop her very charming person into a covered buggy and forcibly elope. It is hardly necessary to say that all this was to be done in the absence of her father. Mr. Jim Wily kindly offered to accommodate his friend **with the** necessary **vehicle.** He was not aware that Howe, during the **entire summer,** had maintained a brave fight against feminine fascinations; notwithstanding a hermit's isolation, and the absolute cessation **of** epistolary hostilities from the fashionably dressed young lady. **He** did not know either, **that** the poor little namesake of **the** illustrious exemplar of Greek conjugal fidelity was in despair of ever hearing from the faithless Howe again, and destitute of any consolation save her owl, now arrived **at** muscular maturity, and apparently anxious **to** emulate the gentleman **by** flying **away.**

The early fall was **at** hand, and **the** rain, so long withheld, charged impatiently upon the exhausted earth, with a fury that left a misty haze **in** the air, like the ghost of a fierce engagement. Amid the violent storm, which **had prevailed** intermittently for five days, Judge Natchez, **returning from** the settlement **of a** local dispute in **a** neighboring **town, received** the news of the **cow-boy's** designs upon his daughter from a transient guest of Jim Wily, who **had** overheard a conversation through **the** sheeting partition of his primitive sleeping-apartment. A Texan hotel is an ambitious rival of the famous Whispering-Gallery.

There was no outburst of profanity on this occasion. He received the details of the plot in that silence which makes intense emotion so awe-inspiring; but the sorry mount of the Judge soon realized that he had never before experienced the possibilities of flagellation nor his own powers to overcome space. In the height of this mad ride, he saw through the encircling mist a buggy, achieving a very comfortable rate of speed along the trail-road between himself and his next neighbor, and proceeding in the direction of the ranch. His face paled; the line of his jaw showed through the tense skin; his knees smote the sides of his horse; but slipping his right arm free from the sleeve of his "slicker," he drew a self-cocking Colt's revolver—the gift of a grateful client, and rode on to intercept him with the sternness of fate.

Rube Smart—for he it was—seeing the Judge, and recognizing him immediately, reined in his horse with his left hand, and, leaning out of the buggy, allowed his right to drop mechanically to his hip. **The gesture** indicated the locality of a weapon—not a self-cocker—but equally speedy in the gentleman's hands. He had long ago filed the notches in the tumbler of the lock, and was wont to discharge it by the mere leverage of his powerful thumb upon the hammer.

A rent in the " slicker " of the horseman disclosed his masked design. Frontier etiquette recognizes no distinction between the drawing of a weapon and its actual discharge ; **the** one implies the other. There were two almost simultaneous reports from within hand-shaking distance. A frantic horse, riderless, and with leaping stirrups, **dashed** wildly away **in the** direction of the ranch. A buggy, from the spinning wheels of which the water flew, went careering madly over the water-soaked prairie. The avenging father and **his** victim lay *dead*, with the **rain** pelting **upon** their ghastly faces.

And even at that moment, Penelope, awaiting anxiously at **the** window her sire's return, marveled **how much** the coursing drops upon the pane resembled tears.

VIII.

ABOUT the time of the occurrence of the trag-
edy mentioned in the last chapter, Mr. Faye
Howe—seated at the stove of the hospitable
Macpherson, a genial Scot whose store was at
once post-office and general base of supplies for
the town of Eden—was engaged in contempla-
tion of his steaming boots, and in cynical meditation upon the inconstancy of woman. The
ring of native Texans around this red-hot dis-
penser of comfort, was practical in its lamen-
tations over the danger of " rises " in the water-
holes and creeks. At each lull in the conversation, the expectorant hiss of the assailed stove
seemed at once to deride and threaten their fears.

Mr. Howe was feeling classical on this occasion ; he was silent, and supported his own experience with the riper judgment of Virgil:—
" Varium et mutabile femina ! " The immediate predisposing cause of so much mental communion and this Latin summary was probably
the receipt that morning of the wedding-cards
of the young lady who has occupied photo-
graphic prominence in these pages. Not that

Mr. Howe was particularly sensitive to the somewhat marked flavor of the lady's social etiquette, but because he reflected with pardonable disparagement upon the apparent readiness with which she had hitherto acknowledged, in notes of superlative perfume and tinted paper, certain gifts of jewelry which his prodigal generosity had in time past felt called upon to tender. It was perfectly human and natural, under the circumstances, that he should dwell with gratified malice upon the far-from-flattering portrait he had formerly drawn of the gentleman who had recently felt called upon to accept such grave responsibilities. It was perhaps the epistolary reflection which led him to dwell with gratified contrast upon the apparent sincerity of Miss Penelope's attachment. Howe was thoroughly conscious of certain *billets-doux*, which—albeit ungrammatical and crippled in orthography—were genuine and unperfumed. A lack of self-prejudice in personal matters made him execrate himself for failure to acknowledge these gratuitous pledges. After this condemnatory introspection he walked to the window. Outside it was raining heavily.

As he stood gazing out at the pouring rain, he was struck by the attitude of resigned fatalism exhibited by his patient steed. The gentleman was conscious of entertaining a peculiar sentiment for this animal. It was not affection, for Howe was singular in *this*, that he had never been able to love any thing which did not first exhibit toward him marked evidence of attachment. Whatever "Oscar" was, he was *not* demonstrative. He had been first attracted to him by that stern practicality which obtains in matters of horse-flesh—his record for speed and endurance. The mustang had been victor in many a prairie "scrub-race," and his fame as a swimmer of unfordable rivers had gone abroad through the county. Later, Howe had come to respect him for his keen instincts. Entering the state with Northern enterprise and that lack of woodcraft proverbial of a "tenderfoot," a carelessness in riding over his boundless "range" had often compelled him to resort to a compass situated in that long barrel head, to prevent passing the night on the bald prairie. Then, a philosophical submission to the inevitable; a stolid patience of misfortune; withal, a serene indifference of

fate had compelled respect. **He** fancifully
believed that the horse reciprocated the sentiment, and that he had faith in his master besides.
This had induced him on one occasion to record
a vehement oath that death alone should **part**
them.

The equine embodiment of so much **good**
sense and appreciation had been the recent
recipient of unusual consolation with **him.**
He had just stored away for future assimilation
six quarts of Texan oats of a quality which **he**
had hitherto doubted **the** state's capacity to
produce.   But his acquaintance **with** that coveted article was remote—his regular dietary
luxury being " corn **in the cob** "—and his brave
heart, although it inhabited no elegant exterior,
was correspondingly cheered. Notwithstanding an unusual accentuation of head and tail-
droop to the rainy weather—of which he, in
common **with** humanity had, of late, experienced **an en**tire sufficiency—it **was** merely in
calm recognition **of** the unalterableness of nat-
ural forces.   " **Oscar** " was **a** pronounced fatal-
ist.   It is quite **possible** that certain reasoning
sentimentalists might have argued from the
humility of his **attitude a** possible prayer of

thankfulness for an unprecedented " square meal." This is entirely a mistake. Mr. Howe glanced over the almost grotesque points of the faithful animal. His ambitious shoulders and unusually long fore-legs suggested the giraffe. Latterly he was mildly inclined to slope. One might have been pardoned in imagining that Nature had contemplated a camelopard, but, having perfected the heart first, was unwilling to place it in the anatomy of any creature except the next to man—the horse. As the gentleman dwelt upon an equine courage that was almost manly, and accepted his suggestion of dripping boot-leather, he was appalled at the sarcasm of calling him " Oscar Wilde." Why was it ? He distinctly saw the animal raise his head and look him full in the face.

A man, pale with excitement, at this moment ran into the store, and announced that he had just found Judge Natchez and Rube Smart lying dead upon the prairie. The door slammed violently. Mr. Howe was gone.

As he loosened the lariat of his mustang he was prompted to look again into his intelligent eyes. What was it he saw there ? Who knows !

Yet as he settled himself in his Mexican saddle,
he felt that sublime **consciousness** of the privileged equestrian—that **horse and master** were
in accord.

That **ride** through flying mud, through
splashing **water, over** the wet prairie! **Here
and** there swollen pools **along** the **way had**
overflowed the trail **in** blank and treacherous
sheets through which his horse dashed **with the
fury** of an angry billow, leaving **the track of**
their fierce progress outlined in flying spray **and**
hurrying curves of bubble and foam. At times
the yielding soil of **the** beaten **track** forced him
to break his way amid chaparral and **copse, and
through thin files of mesquite and live** oak,
standing like **storm-beaten sentinels** in silent
gray, the panting **of his** laboring **steed,** the
cadence **of** plunging hoof-beats swept **by un-**
challenged. As he rode on without whip or
spur, and **felt** the resistless energy **of those**
grand **muscles,** playing like an ʹengine **beneath**
him, he was filled with admiration for his noble
horse.

His watch told **him that the** obscured sun
was **but** "**an hour high**" **as** he passed **the**
pecan motte **and** the dismantled cow-pen **lying**

hidden within its depths. The line of water-holes that he had formerly known was brimming with water, and Nature's chalices seemed eager to burst their emerald cups and overflow the intervening space. He thought of the ranch at the junction of the two creeks—so negligently placed. He thought of the orphaned Penelope. He might yet be too late!

Just as he descended the gaunt divide which sloped gently down to the now visible dwelling, he heard a noise before him, like the wind sighing through thick foliage. He knew it instinctively and caught his breath; the line of water-holes was a foaming creek. Only to his horse's knees as he dashed through it, but he was aware of the danger in those latitudes, and shuddered as he galloped up the little rise and into the live oak clump. Throwing his mustang's bridle over a neighboring post, he ran to the door of the ranch. He knocked. No reply. He knocked again—louder. Silence still. With frontier politeness he turned the knob and entered the young lady's bed-chamber.

The room was twilight dim. Penelope had thrown herself upon the bed and lay asleep. As he entered she opened her eyes wearily, and rose with a sudden flush.

"Why, Faye!" was all she said.

He took the little, brown hands in both his own.

"The creeks are rising, dear; I have come to save you!"

She ran to the window and cast a startled look without; she threw open the door and saw the long flats about the smaller "branch" submerged and threatening; she came back to him with a pallor in her face that Howe had never seen there before. He smiled reassuringly.

"Do not despair," he said. "My sorrel is outside. Are you ready?"

"One moment!" the girl answered, grasping the sombrero dusty with neglect and an old rubber-coat of her father's. She threw them on hastily and ran out into the storm. Howe was left in the little room.

Penelope ran to her little cages; she freed the dove and the mocking-bird, which availed themselves of the privilege. Hesitating a second, she finally drew the confining barriers for the prairie-dog and jack-rabbit; they cowered in their open prisons. Catching up the full-plumaged owl, the faithful little arms attempted to carry him to the horse. The ungrateful wretch fluttered fiercely, broke from her tender clasp, and flapped heavily away. She returned to Howe, who was waiting in the saddle.

He turned his heavy box-stirrup outward a little and reached his right hand to her. Penelope put a trusting little foot on his; she mounted behind him. Two confiding arms were thrown around him. I wot the behavior of the gentleman was in marked contrast to that of the fugitive owl; he displayed no disposition to escape that gentle pressure. Thus they rode out in the brief Southern twilight.

As they descended the slight rise, his heart sank as he saw the larger creek: it was running with the fierceness of a turbulent river,—the current setting with the trend of its valley bed, and, therefore, not always in the middle of the stream. The roaring waters were plunging up the slight declivity *foot by foot*. He glanced back—the lesser branch and its encircling flats were moving rapidly, the tremendous volume of water cutting them off in the rear. The only chance of permanent safety Faye Howe knew was in the great divide, stretching before him dimly like a despairing hope. Something of the desperation of the coming struggle was in him, as he turned in his saddle.

"Little one," he said, throwing a strong arm around her in the gathering twilight, " it is far— far worse than I thought. Your father has not returned. Look at me, darling ! He *never* will, he never *can*. Shall it be mine to take a wife with me to the other side ?"

He felt the pretty brown arms tighten their clasp ; a little head sank upon his shoulder. There came to his listening ear a whisper fragrant with its memories of buffalo clover:

" Faye, I reckon *so*."

He had not hitherto detected the latent poetry of this peculiar Texan idiom.

"Oscar," who had halted upon the sloping declivity as sternly as if carved in stone, immediately shivered and gave a loud snort ; it struck both ominously. Howe leaned forward over his strong neck and patted the animal's ear, very much as an operator taps his telegraphic key. It was an old familiar gesture, understood between them both. The mustang sprang forward and was soon breasting the hurrying flood, but sinking deeper than when the water first swirled around him. Howe disengaged himself from his stirrups, and whispering to Penelope slipped from the saddle, swinging off by the girth. She took his place.

And now the rushing, turbulent river began to bring down on its current fragments of creek-margin and grassy débris. A snake swam past them in tortuous fright. Small sticks of timber drifted sideways with the boiling flood, or shot swiftly past, flying like darts—end-on. The raw-hide-bound cow-pen was breaking up and giving way. Swimming thus on his horse's left, holding on by the saddle-girth, and shielding with his own body the tender limbs of her who was to be his bride, Howe shuddered as he thought of the great pecans. At that instant he heard a loud crash up the creek: his fears were prophetic.

Already under the lee of the great divide he was feeling a rising joy in his heart, when he noticed an uneasy movement of his mustang's head. He strained his eyes through the gloom, but could see nothing. Just as he felt his horse's fore-feet strike the submerged prairie-bottom, a dark, ominous shape, swinging irre-

sistibly with the current on a fulcrum caused
by the resisting bank, struck the brave head of
the noble steed with the force of a thunderbolt.
The stricken neck bowed mutely before the great
destroyer, and with a single convulsive sigh the
doomed animal yielded up his life. The trunk
of a huge pecan that had caught in a side eddy
drifted slowly past and out into the rush of the
whirling creek, like some black and sullen
leviathan. The eternal decree of Fate was
done! But Penelope and Faye, left thus in
the rapidly shoaling water, were saved. The
North and South clasped hands at last.

THE MYSTERY OF SAN SABA.

———o———

DESPONDENCY was rampant at San Saba.
Even at the Crossing, where solemn
pines and ascetic hemlocks hung breathlessly
above the silent river, and threatened with
suicidal tendencies its cloistered gloom, an
atmosphere of discontent infected the reflec-
tive traveler. As he drew near town, this
impression deepened. There was a long line of
heavily saddled horses in front of the " Pasear
House " that had neighed, and bit and kicked
one another dejectly since early morning. Its
querulous proprietor—in spite of these apparent
signs of patronage—was seated idly upon the
front gallery in an attitude of hopeless hypo-
chondria. Unfortunately the opinion of his
guests was skeptical. " Baitin' buzzards,"—the
blacksmith had remarked to an appreciative
audience about his anvil, attracted thither by

the brilliancy of his professional and profane pyrotechnics, and sympathizing with him in the manifest intent to include the daily bill of fare at the Pasear House in his scathing commentary.

The steps about Hackett's Grocery were impassable, in consequence of their freight of long-booted humanity devoted to gloomy whittling and expectoration. The only hilarity available was to be found in the saloons ; and this, being born of alcohol, was uncertain and spasmodic. Joe Treddle, who spent most of his time in making trips on his bicycle between his harness-shop and the bar of the " Two Brothers," as he mounted for the thirteenth pilgrimage, diffused a gloom among the assembled spectators that not even unremitting devotion, since sunrise, to a beverage retailed under the suggestive title of the " Tanglefoot Persuader," seemed likely to dissipate. It was not only the regularity of Joe's potations, but his manner of approaching them, that secured for him the distinction of being the " fastest man in the settlement."

But I hasten to record that the cause of this universal dejection was neither political nor

pecuniary. Since the last election for sheriff,
when the rival candidates had settled the
unpleasantness of a trifling discrepancy in the
returns by an interchange of personal compli-
ments and " six shooters " at the " Two Brothers," and satisfactorily established the claims of
the party most proficient in the use of his
weapon, the harmony of public feeling had been
undisturbed by the sacred privilege of the ballot.
Although in other respects a frontier community, this cheerful application of the modern
doctrine of " survival of the fittest " was at
once recognized as convenient and indisputable.

Nor was the commercial outlook less flattering. The season had been a prosperous one
for stock, and the market prices of wool and
cattle never so generally satisfactory. But
it would seem that there were grievances
beyond the local remedies of municipal serenity and flush times. Miss Cordelia Delancey
was engaged to be married, and the day for the
wedding was at hand. As half the inhabitants
of the town of San Saba and the surrounding
country had been either ardent admirers of
Miss Delancey, or unsuccessful suitors for the

lady's hand, disappointment and despair were epidemic.

It does not necessarily follow that Miss Delancey was either peri or paragon. That she was unquestionably attractive, no one who came within range of her eloquent brown eyes, brilliant color, and fascinating manners could reasonably gainsay. That she was a decided brunette, and that she felt in her own heart a proud consciousness that this fact alone made her more than a match for a dozen sickly and sentimental blondes, were also apparent to the ordinary observer. But when the curious visitor, who had had pulse quickened and imagination fired by tales of this wild rose of the valley, completed his critical inventory of her charms, it was with a conviction that he had met other maidens equally irresistible. Perhaps, had he remained longer, he might have been less positive. For Miss Cordelia possessed the advantage of an unattractive environment, and graced a circle to which the application of the epithet "ornamental" was the language of gallantry rather than fact. And there is abundant testimony that she improved upon acquaintance. It is said that

few were able to resist her deprecatory manner of saying "Now, Mr. Treddle!"; that her
"Yes Sirs," were delicious in their implied
flattery of her auditor; that her very exclamations—the peculiarly feminine one of "Why,
goodness gracious!"—were so musical and
thrilling that they encouraged her less attractive neighbors in a surprising wealth of inter-
jection; and that even the pangs of despised
love and ultimate rejection lost much of their
bitterness by the delicacy of her refusal.

All this may be readily imagined; for Miss
Delancey possessed that rare feminine accomplishment of retaining the friendship of her
unsuccessful suitors, and the town rang with
her praises. She appeared judiciously to curb
the ardent advances of the enamored, to com-
pel a subdued and chastened attitude of
devotion, and from serene and inaccessible
heights to smile sweetly upon the respectful
admiration she elicited.

She had the indispensable requisite of the
successful actress. In a settlement unused to
dramatic influences, Miss Cordelia Delancey
unquestionably—"*drew*." And as she peered
through the shutters of her little room above

the front gallery, **on her bridal** morning, Miss Delancey really **could not** remember, when,—**to** adopt still further **the** forcible language of **the** boards—she had **not** had a "*full house.*" She could **not** remember when the little rail fence across **the road had** not been picturesque with tethered horses, and the front gallery equally picturesque **with** their owners in every attitude **of** hopeless and inthralling passion.

And as she reflected thus—although it **was** her bridal morning—I fear she heaved a tender little sigh—a mere ghost of regret, to be sure, but even so reluctantly does the feminine mind resign the thought of dominion. For those "serene and inaccessible heights," above alluded **to, were** now effectually scaled. At least **it** is not six weeks since Miss Delancey acknowledged **as much**; first, to the young ranchman, Mr. Ridge Johnson, tall, blue-eyed, and blonde-mustached—the living counterpart of Cordelia— on a certain eventful evening in June, **when the** moon, half veiled in clouds, swung **low over the** pines above the **river,** and when, to the **eyes of the** young man **upon** the **front gallery,** the **pale** face, over which the shadows of the honey-suckle drifted, seemed quite as heavenly as the

planet. And second, to old man Delancey—
rough, unlettered, and profane, but not the
least of his daughter's admirers—in the staring,
truthful sunlight of the following morning,
when with crest somewhat lowered, and her
brave, brown eyes a little downcast, she had
presented the gallant of her choice.

"An' so ye reckons to git married, Cordy; to
turn loose an' quit the ole man;" remarked
her father mournfully, as the eyes that had
dwelt mutely upon his daughter's face while
she was speaking, wandered away to the river,
and seemed to gather a vague trouble as he
gazed.—"Wal, I don't say I ain't been ex-
pectin' of it, darter; I ain't a-goin' to 'low but
wot it's nateral an' womanlike, an' dad-blamed
ef ye ain't hed a sight o' temptation too, with all
the boys 'twixt here and Paint Rock cavortin'
'round an' keepin' yer kempeny. But now thet
ye've actooally made a ch'ice"—he paused,
for a certain tremor in the voice, entirely inconsistent with his usual rough manner, had made
his daughter raise her beautiful eyes to his—
"now thet ye've actooally made a ch'ice, it
ain't in me to say thet it don't take the ole
man pretty nigh."

"Why you dear, old, blessed father!" exclaimed Miss Delancey affectionately, taking the old man by the lapels of his ducking jacket, and by this peculiarly feminine style of bondage endeavoring to peer into the dull eyes that resolutely avoided hers,—"you dear, old, blessed, stupid father! You don't suppose Cordy's going to leave you for good and all?"

Whether old Delancey recognized in this womanly appeal the familiar sophistry by which an artful sex attempts to disguise the harshness of existing facts, is debatable, but he evaded the issue by suddenly shifting his ground.

"An' this yer's the shrimp, Cordy, thet you've picked out at last, after all the piany playin' an' goin's on ez hez been into this yer house sence I built it?" he inquired, facing abruptly round with critical practicality, and bringing his disparaging eyes suddenly to bear upon the embarrassed *fiancé*, as if he were a discreditable bullock, or an unpromising sheep;—"this yer's the light-haired shrimp, arter Joe Treddle, an' Blacksmith George, an' Storekeeper Hackett, an' the proprietor of the Pasear, an' all the rest of the likely chaps ez hez been cracked arter you the last six year."

"Wal, dad-burn me fur a tenderfoot, ef gals ain't ez cur'ous an' onsartin ez a Government mule—the best onto 'em, an' thet air a fact!

"Howsomever," he added, after inspecting the abashed young man with pensive deliberation and wide-mouthed astonishment—"ef *yer* taste, Cordy, runs to sorrels an' light colored cattle, I ain't a-goin' to gainsay it. It's you ez is a-gettin' married an' not me, thank God!" (This pious utterance was probably due to a vivid recollection of the infelicity of his own marital experience with the now deceased Mrs. Delancey.) "I was allus tuk with bays and ches'nuts myself, but ef you've laid off to marry this yer cream-colored hoss, I reckon I'll stan' by yer. Them 5,000 head o' steers I promised ye an' the Big Brady Ranch is your'n whenever ye want 'em, so it don't matter much how the young feller is heeled, I reckon. Now I look at him, he's likelier than I reckoned at fust, an' arter all, ye can't allus tell a critter by his color. Shake, son!"

And extending a heavy hand to the astounded prospective son-in-law, the old man welcomed him with a characteristic grip, and the betrothal received the paternal sanction.

This was only six weeks ago, and now the
wedding was imminent. Social events pro-
ceed with rapid strides upon the frontier, where
towns spring up in a night like the palace of
Aladdin. Howbeit, Miss Delancey did not
hasten to pour the tidings of her engagement
into the ear of confiding womanhood, as her
more highly civilized sister would probably have ·
done. A disposition to mutual confidence in
matters of the heart, indulged in at the mature
age of ten, and resulting in premature advertise-
ment among the gossips of the little town, had
made her skeptical in reference to feminine
oaths of secrecy. On the contrary, she kept
the story of her new-found happiness strictly
to herself. But the spectacle of Mr. Ridge
Johnson's mustang, nervously pawing the earth
in solitude before the little rail-fence, and the
conventional—"*Not at home,*"—that social
falsehood which penetrates even the sincerity
of the frontier, soon awakened San Saba to a
realization of the disquieting truth.

Strange to say, the first definite information
came from old Delancey. This was when, after
mature deliberation, he remembered that he
" hed a brother back in Virginny who was the

father o' two darters thet 'lowed to sling more style than any gals in the States, an' he jest nat'rally reckoned now thet *he'd* turn loose an' show 'em." It was then that the demon of social rivalry entered the bosom of Delancey, and he resolved upon issuing " *invites to the weddin'.*" This was no easy task in a community where the etiquette of the process was overlooked in the completeness of the result. Assisted by the editor of the "San Saba Criterion," the following statement was prepared after much thought and study :—

Mr. Reuben Delancey

AT HOME,

At 9:30 A.M. April 20, 1880.

San Saba, Texas.

Miss Cordelia Delancey.   Mr. Ridge Johnson.

When this indefinite announcement of the impending ceremony—printed by the obliging editor upon pink letter-paper—flew North, and surprised the two ultra-fashionable young ladies for whose confusion it had been evolved, its effects were not alarmingly disastrous.

Miss Jessie Delancey—playing tennis with another fashionable young creature of the

opposite sex, who rivaled her in a costume
more appropriate for surf-bathing than any other
obvious use—said she "didn't doubt her Uncle
Rube was home, and she hoped he'd stay there."
Miss Flora, lazily reclining in a hammock upon
the broad veranda, remarked that it was " really
too early in the morning for them to expect her
to call on the old gentleman under the circumstances," and dismissed the matter languidly in
true society fashion.

Howbeit, old Delancey, thousands of miles
away upon the frontier, reflected none the less
complacently upon the convincing proof of
social prestige he had been able to send his
brother's children.

"I reckon thet'll start 'em," he remarked to
Miss Cordelia one afternoon, after a long interval devoted to profound reverie and involuntary
chuckling. "When them gals of Bob's gets
that yer invite I sent 'em, they'll be right smart
of a dust. I kin see yer cousin Flo, who air
old enough, Cordy, to be yer mother, and who
war scarin' all the young fellers by carryin' sich
heavy sail afore I left the States—I kin see her
jest a-tearin' her hair an' a-snatchin' herself
bald-headed from this yer gallery. As fur

Jessie, she ain't no 'count nuther, but she'll be tol'ble riled, I reckon. And what ails them children anyway, Cordy? They don't seem to take with the boys, nohow. Bob's done well 'nuff, but they hain't. An' ef I ain't hed no political honors nur wanted none, I kin buy thet father o' their'n out and twenty like him. I'd jest nat'rally like to know what they air a-gittin' at."

But if old Delancey's imagination was unreliable in estimating the grief of his nieces, there was no disputing its accuracy in matters of material prosperity. Plain in appearance, simple in manner as even the humblest of the many cow-boys he employed, none but an eye skilled in detecting the austerities of the frontier cattle-king would have known him for one of the wealthiest in the State. Yet such was he.

The Big Brady Ranch, already alluded to, lying just fifty miles from San Saba, comprised 200,000 acres of grazing land, well stocked and well watered, and stretching away in rolling billows of prairie without let or limit. It was so vast in extent that it would have taken old Delancey—used as he was to the saddle — four

days of hard riding to encompass his pos-
sessions. Within its limitless confines were
many a hidden cañon and unexplored valley,
where, beneath the staring sun or tremulous
starlight, the buffalo-clover wasted its brooding
incense on the empty air, and the mock-bird
poured out its mad melody to such mute witnesses as the hardy live oak or thorny mesquite
alone ; spots, where the wandering herds that
flecked that chartless, emerald sea seldom pen-
etrated, and the foot of man never ; vast green
silences, overhung by endless blue, and cloudless sylvan solitude, which the wild verbena
embroidered with its pale amethyst, and where
poppyworts spilled their cups of crimson and
gold, and no sound, save the incessant bark of
the marmot, the melancholy pipe of upland plo-
ver, or the gloomy howl of the coyote, broke the
lonely monotony.

And these boundless acres, with 5,000 head
of the stock that roamed them, were to be
Cordelia's. It is probable that this fact had its
weight, and considerably augmented the grief
of the practical community into which old man
Delancey burst one long summer afternoon
with the pink harbingers of the impending

wedding. Land upon the Big Brady was worth two dollars an acre; cattle were selling at thirty dollars a head; the eligible male population of San Saba performed a simple sum in mental arithmetic, and resigned itself to indiscriminate despair.

Miss Delancey had not contemplated the distribution of invitations to her wedding. Being uneducated in that refined cruelty of older civilizations, which sends the rejected suitor the announcement that he is forestalled by a more fortunate rival, she would have spared her late admirers the somewhat marked flavor of modern etiquette. No such scruples actuated her sire. After the example of Holy Writ—albeit unconsciously — he went forth into the highways and hedges, and personally bade to the wedding. Nor were the recent aspirants to the hand of his daughter slighted in this generous hospitality.

" I hope ye'll all come, an' hev a gin'ral tear 'round," he said with great liberality of manner, as he distributed the last of his social favors among the bibulous patrons of the " Two Brothers."

" There'll be no end o' fun, and Cordy an'

me allows, in course, there's to be no hard
feelin's among the chaps ez she's left out.
Everythin's fair in love and brandin' cattle.
Don't care ef I do, Joe, on this festive occasion.
My reg'lar pizen," he remarked cheerfully to the
bartender, on being requested by Mr. Treddle
to emulate him in his persistent patronage.
"Ez I'm on this yer subjek," he said easily,
resting one elbow on the bar and turning his
dull eyes on his attentive auditors—" I may as
well let on that I means to do things up in
shape while I'm 'bout it, by givin' of a barbecue, an' out o' respect fur ole times—
'Whisky'll be *free* in the back room.'"   This
generous announcement—a tribute to the
method by which old Delancey had laid the
foundation of his fortune when a mere country
storekeeper in a neighboring settlement—was
received with applause and acclamation.

The long anticipated morning dawned in
brilliant apotheosis of crimson and gold upon
the eastern horizon, that later grew into the
effulgent sun. As the long lances of light
slipped above the summits of the low hills,
and shivered themselves in a dazzling sortie
upon the glittering landscape, signs of prepara-

tion were visible about the " Delancey House."
The posts of the front gallery were wreathed
and garlanded with mistletoe from the neighboring valleys, and the spacious frame-house
wore an air of unusual hospitality. The Texan
barbecue, in its incipient stages, was exemplified by large fires on the level in front of the
dwelling, and an ox roasting whole. Around
these beacons of coming good cheer, the vol-
unteer cooks of the locality busied themselves
and bustled. Early as was the hour the guests
were arriving, and the clanking of spurs and the
creaking of expostulatory wheels startled the
still morning air. A long ride of fifty miles lay
before bride and bridegroom; for, in consequence of the need of supervision at the Big
Brady Ranch, their future home was to be the
terminus of the customary wedding trip.

Within the ample parlors the country side
from far and near assembled—conspicuous
among which, the disconsolate contingent of
the fair Cordelia's suitors, fortified against outward expression by repeated draughts of that
panacea for human ills already advertised as
available in the back room—awaited expect-
antly the coming of the bride.

She came presently. Certainly no fairer had
the morning dawned over the San Saba hills
than Cordelia upon that enraptured audience,
blushing as the conscious East, with brown
eyes, swept on either cheek by downcast lashes,
and leaning on the arm of her blonde Hype-
rion. So radiant was her lovely presence, that
notwithstanding the precautionary measures
against expressive emotion above alluded to,
a very audible and alcoholic sigh was exhaled
from various quarters of the room, and Joe
Treddle, with an involuntary gesture of despair, left the room abruptly, and spent the time
occupied by the ceremony in solitary communion with the counter-irritant in the back room.

The brief rites by which matrimony is solemn-
ized upon the frontier were quickly over, and
the fair Cordelia was resigned to the congratu-
lations of admiring friends. It was hardly ten
o'clock by old Delancey's shagreen-cased watch,
when, escorted to the gate with much effusive
demonstration, she took her seat in the square,
light carriage in waiting, and as Mr. Ridge
Johnson gathered up the reins and cracked his
whip, a shower of rice, and several antiquated
slippers of frontier pattern, accompanied the

happy couple part way upon their wedding
journey. The exuberant guests, having discharged their congratulatory duties with well
counterfeited zeal, devoted themselves immediately with greater zest to the substantial good
cheer awaiting them upon the front lawn.
Throughout the long afternoon the fierce sun
brooded over a noisy, convivial, and perspiring
throng; but Reuben Delancey, busying himself in profuse hospitality toward his many
guests—albeit a little unsteady upon his pins
from repeated toasting of the bride—was conscious of an overmastering feeling of bereavement and loss that resisted even repeated stimulation; and once the old man found himself in
a corner of his grounds, gazing vacantly in the
direction of the River Crossing, and dashing a
tear or two from his shaggy lashes with his
hirsute hand.

Toward nightfall black clouds came troop-
ing over from the west, obscuring the drooping
sun, and later a thunderstorm of unusual violence descended upon guests and host. As
they fled from its fury into the spacious mansion, and listened to the crash of the lurid
bolts that cleft the startled air, and the sharp

fusillade of the driving rain, a strange fancy
that the elements were in sympathy diffused
itself in the minds of all. It was at once as
if Nature reciprocated and reproduced the tears
of the father, and the imprecations of the rejected suitors over the recent union.

A week elapsed—a week of peculiarly depressing weather, even in that monotonous and level
landscape. A cold, shroud-like mist clung
about the shoulders of the low hills that at
night slipped down their flanks, and stole with
ghostly footfall through the damp and dreary
town. All day long the leprous sycamores
about the stagnant pools were restless as with
a nervous dread, and the sallow willows convulsed, distracted, and hysterical. In the leaden
atmosphere the somber ranks of evergreen at
the Crossing seemed like mourners bending
reverently above an enormous grave, and the
rush of the writhing river, far below, came like
a smothered sob from the black abyss.

And then, one day, a horseman spurred his
laboring steed into the foaming current, scram-
bled breathless and dripping up the steep
opposite bank, and dashed rapidly away over
the flat road to the Delancey house. It was

Delancey's old and experienced foreman, and he brought with him a strange story. There had been no arrival of the expected bride and bridegroom at the Big Brady Ranch.

For a brief interval the mind of the fond father was occupied with surmise and conjecture of some possible mishap. "Thet 'ar dadburned mustang 'Bolero' might have slipped his hobbles an' lit out in the night across country," he ruminated. "But even so, they cud ha' footed it to Brady," was his instant reflection.

By degrees the puzzled expression with which he had received the news gave way to one of uneasiness, and then of absolute anxiety, until, grasping his heavy cow-hat and riding-whip, he sprang up behind his foreman, and together they galloped to the "Pasear."

A hurried consultation with its querulous proprietor followed. But as that worthy had not yet emerged from his hygienic slough of despond, it did not contribute to alleviate his apprehension, and when the untimely ringing of the great hotel bell startled the scattered guests a few minutes later, a general alarm speedily spread throughout the village. From

far and near, as at the beat of an alarming
drum, the men assembled: the blacksmith
bearing a red hot iron, hastily plucked from the
forge; Hackett with the cheese-knife, with which
he had been serving a customer, still redolent
of its employment; Joe Treddle, hopelessly
drunk upon a reeling and erratic bicycle,
bringing up an inglorious rear with a disastrous "header."

The story was soon told. In that country
of quick resolve and instant execution, decision
was not wanting. Although the "Wild Rose"
had been plucked by the hand of another, she
still held for all a subtle and vicarious charm.
Even his spirituous disguise did not conceal the
solicitude of Joe Treddle.

"Mish Cordy nosh shone hup," hiccoughed
the irresponsible Joe,—"nosh at 'ome—wass
mäar—wass mäar, ole man? She 'ere, boys,
lesh fine 'er—thash was mus' do—ri' 'way—no
time loosh—I shay, mus' fine 'er rish hoff!"

A shout of approbation drowned this maudlin
logic. By noon, a motley cavalcade, armed to
the teeth, heavy-spurred, and big-sombreroed,
had left the town behind them, and were away
upon the trail. Far in front, pale, rigid, and

staring-eyed, the father, mounted upon a fleet mustang, followed the faint and fading tracks ; and far in the rear, rubicund, relaxed, and bleared, but still potent, struggling onward with a common purpose, Joe Treddle reeled in his saddle.

Little heart have I to follow them on that despairing search ; to recount that agonizing quest through valley and cañon. Skills it little now the telling, how, traced through yielding sand and resisting gravel, the trail grew fainter, fainter, until, washed by recent rains and woven with the hoof-prints of countless stock, it vanished altogether; nor later, when the intelligent scrutiny with which the search began gave way to fortuitous inquiry and chance reconnoitering over that inland ocean, how the blank desert waste rang with cracking "Winchesters" and exploding "Colts," fired in signal. Seven days, from dawn to twilight, they sought the Wild Rose of San Saba. Seven nights, beneath a delirious and gibbous moon, the uncertain curtain of the night was rent with the red flashes and shattering reports of fire-arms, and the leaping flames of torch and pine-knot frightened the gaunt coyote from afar.

But the grim stillness gave no answering sign
The undulating prairie billows rolled away
against the vague horizon; the live oaks
stretched their sturdy limbs to heaven, and the
drooping mesquites bent their heads in ominous
salutation. The vast, measureless, illimitable
solitude was reticent of its agonizing secret still.

When at last, worn out with ineffectual inquiry and fruitless effort, the mounted throng
dispersed, none but the heart-broken father was
left behind at the Big Brady Ranch. A faint
hope—feeble, despairing, still kept him on his
quest. The earliest throb of the morning star
found him in the saddle, and the startled jack-
rabbit, plunging wildly from its form, beheld
him up and away. When a fortnight later,
pale, leaden-eyed, dejected — a mere emaciated
ghost of the bustling, energetic old man that
had regaled them a month since — he rode
slowly into San Saba, it was understood that
he too had abandoned the search.

And so the weeks passed; summer lapsed
into autumn—the long harrow of the wild goose
dragged ceaselessly across gray skies, and their
dusky squadrons were jubilantly discordant in
creek and meadow; autumn faded into winter

—the sudden Northers swept down from Kansas
with their ice pageantry and blinding sleet ; and
still no word, no sign. Meanwhile, the faint
hope that still flickered in the bosom of the
bereaved old man faded also, and gave place
to helpless despair. He had changed pitifully
with the failing year. His dull eyes—always
irresponsive—were now vacant and wandering;
the sturdy shoulders were bowed beneath their
weight of grief; the hair—of late years streaked
with gray—had grown nearly white. Every
thing about him bore the imprint of his absorbing sorrow.

When the spring opened, he bade farewell
forever to town-life, and, parting from his associates with a perfunctory shake of the hand,
betook him to his ranch upon the Big Brady.
Here, with no society save the rough men
he employed, three long, monotonous years
dragged by. As he grew older, he lost his frank
hospitality, and becoming more than ever engrossed in the business of stock-raising, grew
querulous and crabbed. It was as if the calamity
that had overtaken him, had made him distrust-
ful of all things. He essayed the somewhat
dangerous experiment of running sheep and

cattle side by side, and his enormous range was now pasturing ten thousand Merino sheep.

In the mean time the slow years had wrought their changes in the village of San Saba. The proprietor of the " Pasear " had been at last absorbed by his hygienic slough, and slept peacefully in the little cemetery by the river, beneath the funereal pines. The blacksmith and the storekeeper had taken other Roses to themselves—albeit less lovely and less besought —and were now rejoicing in a juvenile parterre of buds and blossoms. Joe Treddle—finding the pursuit of harness-making incompatible with his incessant patronage of the Two Brothers—had turned his attention to politics with gratifying success. After an unusually vinous canvass, he was elected County Judge, and the Concho Circuit became at once famous for incoherent articulation and dubious legal precedent.

As the judicial dignity grew upon him, he proved the healing powers of time by selecting a widow with whom to share the honors of his new condition. His lady's assumption of the title of Mrs. Judge Treddle was none the less emphatic from the fact that she had commenced

her social career as cook in a sheep-camp. Perhaps it was his helpmate's knowledge of this
industry that led his Honor eventually to
undertake it. When the sheep-men began to
organize—the better to protect their interests
—the popularity of the genial Judge enabled
him to secure the additional distinction of
" Delegate from Concho Co., for the Prevention
of Scab." It was this additional responsibility
which sent him once a year to Austin, to represent with maudlin rhetoric before the " Wool
Growers' Convention," the urgency of keeping
in quarantine all diseased flocks; it was this
which invariably impelled him, on the way
back, to purchase sheep at a suspiciously low
figure and drive them recklessly through the
country in furtherance of the truth of his
remarks; and it was the possession of a homicidal negro as herder—whom the Judge's legal
authority had enabled him to acquit already of
several murders—that had hitherto prevented
the sheep-men of Concho Co. from forcibly
opposing his triumphant and pastoral return.
Altogether the rise of the genial judge into
power and prominence had been peculiarly
brilliant and edifying.

It was a bright, clear day at the Big **Brady Ranch.** The **westering sun was** lording **it as** usual over the stifling landscape, warping that spacious structure into sharp crepitation, and causing the pine boards **to exude a** tearful and resinuous remonstrance from the fierceness of **its** oppression. The small, red lizards that were **wont,** during the long hours of the afternoon to **seek the** shadow of its eastern eaves, **were** enjoying **an** unusual immunity from molestation. The hands were all away upon the range. Only old Delancey, **in a corner of** the ample dooryard, **busy in doctoring certain ailing** ewes of his **"hospital flock," was left** behind to **appreciate the general loneliness and** desolation.

When, therefore, the clicking of **the** ranch-gate, and the rattling of a windlass, bore evidence that some strolling cow-boy was availing himself of the refreshment of the well, he strolled over to the curb with weary steps and a gruff "Howdy."

"**How's stock over on Maverick?"** he inquired, **recognizing the new comer,** and sitting **down** negligently upon a neighboring nail-keg.

"Jes' tol'ble!" replied the cow-boy—a blonde Hercules, encumbered by the huge leggings of his calling,—"jes' tol'ble! I reckon I counted nigh onto seven likely calves 'twixt here and the fork—all dead from screw-worm."

"I wanter know!" ejaculated old Delancey with despondency appropriate to the intelligence,—"*I wanter know!* 'Pears like ez ef every thin' this yer season war dad-burned an' dod-rotted! I lost nine steers this brandin' from them 'ere 'tarnal flies; them Febooary lambs was all pizened on laurel—*swelled up*, by thunder and snakes! keeled over, an' died without a blate—an' now here's the calves a-goin'! It do seem," he went on with increasing impatience, "as ef thet thar devil from hell war into things, an' thet air a fact! 'Pears like ez ef the only thing I hev to be thankful fur is thet I ain't got the scab, and thet air suthin', when they tell me they're jest a drappin' down in McCulloch Co. like manner into the wilderness."

"An' ye won't be outer thet long, nuther," responded the gloomy cow-boy, ignoring Delancey's theology. "Ez I kem across thet strip of purrara over by Yoho's this mornin'—an hour afore sun, I reckon—I seen thet thar Jedge

Treddle, jest back from Austin, a-drivin' the scabbiest flock o' sheep I ever seed right across yer range. The Jedge an' his woman were in a hack, an' thet bloody nigger o' his'n an' a greaser on horseback were a-junein' 'em along over the western divide. The sheep was plum red with scab, and a-layin' down every minit and a-scratchin'. If them big wethers o' your'n come within a mile o' there, they'll ketch it, sartin."

Old Delancey sprang up at this information, livid with rage and trembling with passion.

" Wot's thet yer sayin'?" he screamed. " Is thet thar drunken Joe Treddle comin' 'cross my range, spite'n all I've tole him, an' Hackett jes' sendin' me word he's all out o' thet sheep-dip! Here, Jack! Rube! Aleck! saddle ' Bother-'em ' an' load them ' Winchesters ' right smart!"

Then remembering that he was alone on the ranch, he stopped abruptly.

Howbeit, the news was too urgent to allow him to be long silent. After some moments devoted to picturesque and sulphurous characterization of Judge Treddle's genealogy, and a forcible expression of preference for being that instant where patience **and** persistence in his **blasphemous vocabulary would doubtless land him** eventually, **he** hurriedly loaded his " Winchester " and " six-shooters," saddled his **mustang,** and calling **to his** cow-boy informant, **set** out for the scene of **his** animadversions.

After a long gallop **over** the rolling prairie, he overtook the legal gentleman and his woolly cohorts, slowly journeying westward. It was **indeed as the** cow-boy **had said. The** frantic **sheep** dragged their wretched bodies wearily **along,** stopping ever and anon to lie down **and** roll**, or** to bite and tear their mangy **fleeces.** Shaking with passion, Delancey rode up.

" Howdy ! " exclaimed the genial Judge, extending an **uncertain** hand and a more or less inebriated person from the **hack.** " Fac' ish I'se glad shee yer, D'lanshey—I am, thash fac' ! Git down ! git **down ! git in the hack ! "**

Ignoring this cordial invitation and the beam**ing** presence **of Mrs.** Treddle, seated impressively by the side of her bibulous spouse, Delancey broke out :

" **I reckon** I've hed jest 'bout all I care fur o' this yer bizness, Jedge—jes 'bout all I care fur. **Do you call** this sort o' thing **neigh**borly, driv-

ing scabby sheep over my range without givin'
me warnin'?"

"Wal, no!" said the judicial presence, smiling benignly from the hack, and striving in vain
to bring his swaying body face to face with the
emergency. "Can't shay zhackly nayboorly—
thash fac'!—shame time, D'lanshey, we'sh ole
fren's—you'n me's ole fren's—git down!—wass
määr?—them sheep's all ri'!—wass määr?—lesh
ha' drink."

And the Judge produced a black bottle from
under the seat, and held it out with unsteady
fingers and maudlin hospitality toward Delancey.

But the old man was now beyond alcoholic
propitiation.

"Look here! Judge Treddle," he almost
screamed, "this yer thing hez got to stop right
here, d'ye understand?—*right here!*—or there'll
be a differ. It'll cost me nigh onto three thousand dollar to dip my sheep, an' ef they git the
scab I'll hev the money outer yer hide, or I'll
die fust! What's more," he added ominously,
laying a heavy hand on the handle of a revolver, "ef you or any o' yer outfit is on my
range by sun-up to-morrer mornin', ye'll stay

there fur cullinders—*fur cullinders*, d'ye understand?" he shrieked.

With which graphic simile of the direness of
the vengeance that awaited the intruding party,
he subsided.   Judge Treddle received the edict
with effusion,

"All ri'! D'lanshey, ole boy!   Hoo-roar!
hoo-roar!!   Talksh like book—thash law!" he
said, beaming down upon his wife with judicial
dignity.   "D'lanshey a'mos' lawyher — thash
fac'!"

Then suddenly changing his expression and
leaning from the vehicle with a drunken leer,

"Don't you reckon yoosh besher be gittin'
back to ransh?"

All the pent up wrath of Delancey blazed up
and burst forth at this implied suggestion of
ordering him off his own range.   In an instant
he had drawn a revolver.   A wild, murderous
desire to shoot the drunken trespasser dead in
his tracks, surged through his brain.   The next
moment the long, blue barrel of a "Winchester"
in the hands of the homicidal black, whose
eyes were rolling with excitement, stayed his
hand.

"I'se got you, Mass' D'lancey! I'se got you

sure nuff !" grinned the homicide, covering the
old man with the rifle.

Delancey recognized the logic of the situation ; he restored his weapon to its holster.
Without a word he wheeled his mustang
sharply around and galloped off, followed by
the cow-boy.

But not without malediction or anathema.
As his fleet pony put rod upon rod between
him and the trespassers, the enormity of their
transgression found vent in the resources of a
forcible—if not a strictly elegant—vocabulary.
Amid a wealth of lurid metaphor and graphic
invective, the cow-boy gathered that they
were both upon the brink of revolting and
indiscriminate bloodshed of the most appalling
kind.

Thus riding rapidly—the old man still breathing out threatenings and slaughter—they came
suddenly upon a thorny chaparral, into which,
without pausing to skirt it, they furiously
dashed. For a few moments nothing was
heard save the plunging and rearing of their
horses, as they burst their way through the
thick and tangled underbrush, when all at once
old Delancey's mustang sank suddenly to the

ground, throwing him violently from the saddle.
He was on his feet in an instant, cursing the
luckless brute which had stepped into a marmot
burrow and slipped her shoulder. An ominous flapping of wings caused both to look up.
Suddenly the form of the old man became fixed
and rigid, his bloodshot eyes, set and staring.
In this attitude he remained motionless, with
outstretched hand pointing through the thicket.
The eyes of his companion followed the gesture.

There, in a small opening beyond, weather-
beaten and bedraggled—its hangings moldy
and torn—its wheels rusty and crumbling—
with one shattered door hanging helplessly
from a broken hinge—a square, light carriage
was dimly visible. Both rushed to the spot.
It needed not the peculiar fashion of the side-
lamps ; the tattered corduroy cushions ; the
heavy harness, dry and hard from exposure to
the weather, lying like the folds of an anaconda
about a heap of whitened, equine bones, to
identify that ruined conveyance. The mind of
Delancey leaped at once to a realization of the
awful and overwhelming truth. A neighboring
live oak, smitten into desolate ruin by the

ruthless thunderbolt; the shivered door; the gloomy buzzards, perched like unclean spirits of disaster upon adjacent boughs, were all unmistakable witnesses of an appalling doom. When, at length, they summoned courage to disturb the ruins of that four-wheeled sepulcher, the evidences of universal death were not many but indisputable. A heavy riding-boot, shrunken and distorted; a rein hanging over the dashboard, just as it had fallen from the nerveless hand that held it; a tattered glove and ribbon; some shreds of clothing; and a few moldering bones that the prowling wolves and birds of prey had spared, were all that remained of the Wild Rose and her husband.

THREE STREPHONS OF CONCHO.

---o---

IT was hot upon the South Brady. The advent
of an early Texan spring had been unusually
aggressive. To the dwellers by the narrow line
of creek, the daily lances of the sun seemed to
charge relentlessly upon the scanty foliage that
fringed and dotted the little valley. They
pierced the thorny corslets of the mesquites
and forced from the arms of the live oaks the
dusky pennons they had borne triumphantly
in the face of blustering Northers. Only the
birds seemed jubilant over the forward season.
The mocking-birds, indeed, wantoned from
spray to spray, filling the air with their delirious
ventriloquism, and the sentinel scissor-tail bared
his rosy bosom joyfully to the invading sunlight ; but the flocks at noon sought the feeble
shade complainingly ; the prairie-dogs deprecated the heat in shrill barks from their many

burrows; even the rattlesnakes resigned all communion with nature, save at evening or early dawn.

Apparently, the enervating influences of the weather were appreciated by the proprietors themselves. Although the lambing season was near at hand, they were not visible around the ranch nor in the neighboring sheep-pens. All work in preparation for that busy time seemed to have been suspended or abandoned. The primitive brush inclosure had been subdivided into many small corrals by thin partitions and wicket gates ; a few narrow cribs, made of criss-crossed rails, awaited the occupancy of refractory ewes. Several newly-fashioned shepherds' crooks leaned against the gate, and a bundle of rustic paint-brands lay in a corner. All human responsibility for these industrious efforts was evidently hidden from view in the little cabin.

Indeed, the laziness of its occupants suggested apathy. The "Cook" lay asleep in a *negligée* of apparel and attitude quite shameless and characteristic. The "Oracle," who was recognized by that title as a reluctant authority upon the sheep question, was engaged in cutting up a plug of "natural leaf," preparatory to filling his pipe. The " Deacon "—a sobriquet inspired by the gentleman's customary reticence—was listlessly cracking and eating pecans upon the doorstep. By the single narrow window the " Old Man "—a synonym of seniority rather than age—was occupied in the perusal of a recently received letter. A general atmosphere of passive lassitude pervaded the group.

"Well, boys," said the Old Man, with a sigh, as he slowly folded his letter and replaced it in its envelope, "I reckon she 's likely to pay us a visit."

" Who 's *she ?* " inquired the Oracle, striking a match.

"My daughter Kate."

Evidently the reply caused his auditor some surprise, for he allowed his match to go out.

"Wh-a-t !" said he, with a stare of amazement.

" Here, Cook! brace up and have some style about you! Don't you hear that lovely woman is going to visit the ranch ? "

The individual thus roughly addressed sat up, lazily rubbing his eyes.

"The Old Man's daughter's coming down," explained the Oracle.

"Nice accommodations and surroundings for a lady," replied the Cook, in a sarcastic tone. "Pleasant landscape," he added, with a dejected wave of the hand toward the open door.

The Oracle raised his eyes at the gesture. A wild steer, engaged in satisfied mastication of a pair of ducking overalls lately discarded by the speaker, monopolized the near vista.

"That's what I said in my last," retorted the Old Man, apologetically. "I told her I reckoned a sheep-camp weren't naturally no kind o' place for her this time o' year; but women is onsartin, and Kate's bound to come. She says she's lonely up to Paint Rock, and ain't got no society at this season on account of the 'round-ups,' and thet we needn't sling on any extra style on her account."

"Don't you suppose you could persuade her to postpone this trip of hers until I can get to see my tailor?" inquired the Oracle, gazing despondently at his ragged frontier dress.

"Or until I've finished my regular six weeks' washin', said the Cook, with a rueful glance at the wash-tub, on which he had recently suspended hostilities.

The Deacon said nothing, but quietly raised

one foot, and introduced the yawning side of a mendicant boot into the dialogue.

"No," said the Old Man, with an air of resig-nation. "I reckon she 'lows to come, and the only thing we can do is to make the best of it. We'll hev to quit campin' out in this yer room and fix it up for her accommodation. You boys kin raise thet thar tent thet's out in the barn, and I'll do my sleepin', I reckon, in the kitchen. We'll try an' make out some-how."

"But how do you reckon a young lady'll stand washin' in a tin basin, and livin' on bacon and beans?" suggested the Cook.

"Wal," said the Old Man, slowly, "ef a gal will come whar she ain't wanted, and can't stand it arter she gets thar, why, she's got to, thet's all."

Having delivered himself of this logical state-ment, with the air of a judge pronouncing a de-cision from which there can be no appeal, this inconsiderate father raised himself upon a pair of legs, wofully rheumatic and uncompromising at the knees, and picking up his battered hat, stumped pensively away upon these animated stilts in the direction of the sheep-pen.

The trio left behind regarded the situation
with cynical disfavor.   Each individual, being
thoroughly conscious of the degradation of his
own garments, took an ironical pleasure in
gratuitous concern for the wardrobe of his
friends. The Cook devoted himself to the
washing of his dishes, and the clearing away of
a sketchy repast, of which they all had recently
partaken, after gravely expressing the hope that
the Oracle would avoid shocking the finer feelings of their prospective guest by sewing up
various rents in his apparel.   The peculiar
quality of the Cook's solicitude was somewhat
heightened by the fact that he was himself rejoicing in the untrammeled freedom of a net-
ting shirt.   The Deacon's forebodings for the
Oracle were apparently of a moral character.

"I'd recommend ye," said he, for the first
time breaking his silence, and addressing that
individual, "to be more particular hereafter
about cussin' when yer bringin' in them late
ewes about sun-down.   I can always tell where
ye are by the brimstone comin' down the
wind."

"Deacon," said the Oracle very solemnly, with
a disparaging finger directed to the gentle-

man's vagabond feet, "it always went against me to take the advice of a man whose boots were laughing at him."

Howbeit, a generous rivalry prevailed among them to make themselves and their abode presentable to the eyes of a critical and fastidious sex. It is not written, the degree of discomfort men will cheerfully endure, provided the poverty of their surroundings be not exposed to feminine scrutiny. The daughter of the Old Man had hitherto occupied in the minds of all a mythical existence. He had never alluded to her but once before, and then in such a vague and general way as to provoke a pardonable skepticism in his auditors. It was at the last shearing—a time when the entire "outfit" at the ranch was overburdened with work—that the Old Man had suddenly developed an untoward desire to visit his daughter, and had persisted in adhering to it in spite of all efforts to persuade him to the contrary.

Upon his return to the camp, a slight and ironical cross-examination to which he had been subjected by his partners, had been sustained by that worthy with commendable fortitude, and by degrees the occurrence had been forgotten amid the monotonous duties of their daily lives. Roused now by his sudden announcement into spasmodic anxiety for outward appearances, they developed a surprising energy.

A slight inspection of the externals of American sheep-ranches is calculated to impress the observer unfavorably. It would seem that civilized man, as he retrogrades toward barbarism, develops attributes common to lower animal life. To leeward of these arks of human progress are found degraded articles of ephemeral adornment, so shamelessly abandoned as to suggest the discarded sloughs of some hitherto unclassified reptilian. A life, so near to nature's heart, apparently imbues its beneficiaries with unexampled charity, for a reckless prodigality is shown in the contribution of cast-off clothing. An exceptional immunity from the privileges of female society had made the gentlemen of the South Brady phenomenal in this regard, and a commendable prudence in the manipulation of a querulous wheelbarrow, was necessary to remove these gratuitous donations to a remote locality. Appropriate attention was also devoted to an apparent ubiquity on the part of empty tin cans, as imparting to the surrounding landscape a vagrant picnic suggestion.

But it was to the interior of the little cabin that their efforts at rejuvenation were most directed. An endeavor was manifest on the part of the ranchmen to eradicate all traces of former masculine occupancy. In this they perhaps followed a latent impulse of the sterner sex to idealize woman in proportion as her personality is less frequent. Howbeit, the gradual accumulations of masculine débris were all satisfactorily removed, and the walls cleared of a picturesque and warlike tenantry. A small cot-bed was reared in one corner, and every possible effort made contributory to personal comfort. And then the hand of utility was superseded by that of art, and the Oracle's taste for decoration was displayed. The rude interior was illuminated by the flash of birds' wings; and the plumage of green-winged teal, and red-shafted flicker, and prairie bird-of-paradise vied with one another in imparting to the room a gay and *bizarre* appearance. Two pairs of small deer antlers were furnished by the Cook and securely fastened to the walls—

a species of hat and clothes-rack much affected upon the frontier; and when the neighboring valleys had contributed several knots of wild verbena and buffalo-clover, their faint perfume seemed already anticipatory of feminine presence.

But I think it was in personal matters that the gentlemen most palpably acknowledged the speedy advent of the Old Man's daughter. This was evinced by extraordinary solicitude and in a manner entirely characteristic of each. The Cook—although the recipient of unusual license in costume at the hands of his companions on account of the peculiarly trying nature of his duties—had of late been given over to unpardonable *abandon.* This apparent shamelessness had resisted all appeal or criticism on the part of his associates, but now yielded gracefully in favor of their prospective visitor. Impelled by that inevitable law of extremes which attends all social revolutions, his subsequent decorum of dress even went so far as to adopt a small paper cap, which he invariably wore while attending to all matters of the *cuisine.* A surprising daintiness also possessed him in the preparation of articles for the table,

Appetites upon the frontier are too keen to be fastidious. He who caters to them feels that he has but two requisites to fulfill. If meals are forthcoming at the appointed hour, and in sufficient *quantity* to appease the customary vacuum, there is little complaint. A consciousness of this fact, together with the somewhat tedious character of the gentleman's labors, had made him of late quite careless and perfunctory. But now the beans must be carefully assorted and frequently washed; the bacon was invariably treated to a hot-water bath before frying—a process hitherto omitted, ostensibly for fear of destroying the flavor, and the proportions of soda and shortening in the preparation of bread were scrupulously adhered to.

In consequence of these efforts the monotonous viands developed a refinement and relish hitherto unknown.

At the same time the position of the Cook, as chief magistrate of the domestic bureau at the ranch, encouraged him to introduce certain innovations in table etiquette characteristic of his political bias for civil service reform. He required the performance of ablutions before presentation at table, and endeavored to make this measure popular by himself setting the example. The gentlemen were also urged to adopt the revived conventionalism of wearing coats at meals, the Deacon being publicly request-ed not to eat with his knife ; and then, having with infinite pains succeeded in manufacturing a set of napkins out of a piece of cotton "sheet-ing," this social mentor, from his position at the head of the festive board, requested their sub-sequent use, and an entire discontinuance of the former demoralizing habit of improvising nap-kins of their trowsers' legs as imparting an alto-gether untidy personal appearance.

The preliminaries resorted to by the Oracle were entirely those of dress, and were limited to the rather ostentatious wearing of a highly starched and boldly checked pink shirt, inflict-ing upon the beholder by the ambitious roll of its collar, an unusually long and bilious neck. Unremitting attention, however, to a guitar that had long hung neglected above his couch, and by its vagabond appearance and relaxed and broken strings seemed to argue the decadence of Euterpe's worship at the ranch, together with repeated calls upon a certain "Jennie," to await the " rolling by " of seemingly distressing "clouds," and an apparent desire to inflict the superfluous fact that there was a "lovely little spot down in Southern Tennessee," were not without filling his companions with forebodings that the Oracle was contemplating a serenade. As the musical efforts of the Oracle were not attended with that harmony which the melodious instrument might seem to imply, a feeling of mild despondency at this juncture pervaded the camp.

Whatever change in mode of life was contemplated by the Deacon seemed to be entirely restricted to personal cleanliness. That reticent individual at once developed a tendency to bathe twice a day and rigidly adhered to it. As his performance of this ceremony was quite public, his comrades were divided between skepticism and alarm as to what course he would elect upon the arrival of their guest, but eventually came to regard his idiosyncrasy as a peculiar propitiatory observance. Having discarded his mendicant boots for a more presentable pair, he proceeded to grace his left foot with a large silver spur, which, in spite of abundant ridicule, he thereafter persisted in wearing. Whether he affected this singular

appendage because he fancied that it gave him
a general flavor of the cavalier, or whether he
adopted it as a means of urging forward future
dilatory ewes, was a matter of ungratified
curiosity at the little camp, for on this subject
the Deacon preserved his customary reticence.

In such characteristic fashion were their
various preparations made. And then, as if in
recognition, there slipped benignly through the
gates of Dawn a succession of days so mild and
calm, filling the flowering prairie with a joy so
beatific, a peace so infinite, that it rested
upon their labors, like Heaven's benediction,
and at the close of one of these perfect days, an
equestrian footfall startled the dwellers by the
little creek, and rushing from their humble
cabin they beheld a lovely apparition framed
against the golden sunset. So gracefully this
apparition sat her horse, so lovely did she look
in the hush of the gloaming, that, I wot, it was
with a feeling akin to worship that the men un-
covered, and beheld her spring from her horse,
crying, " Well, father, I reckon I've got here
at last !"

And there was little doubt she had. For
when they had overcome the first awkwardness

of their meeting with a proverbially bewildering sex, and it had further transpired that this
divinity was dangerously gracious; that she
was charmed with the result of their efforts in
her behalf; and that—in a manner thoroughly
superficial and maidenlike—she declared immediately that she believed ranching must
be "just too lovely for any thing"—these rude
bachelors of Concho County straightway fell to
adoring her, each after his separate fashion.   I
know not how to account satisfactorily for this
singular idolatry. Perhaps their long exemption
from feminine influences made the gentlemen
unusually susceptible.   But I have to record
that, in her radiant presence, they were speedily
overcome with a sense of their entire unworthi-
ness to consort with so charming a creature;
that the young lady was not slow to perceive
her ascendency; and that, after the manner of
Circe of old, the siren soon transformed them
into abject and willing slaves.

It was not long before " Miss Kate," as they
all called her, began to blight the sociability of
her attendant knights. Hitherto there had
been a remarkable unanimity of feeling in the
little camp, and much good humor and a

general tolerance of individual foibles had prevailed. ·Now, however, in proportion as she
lavished the charm of her society upon one or
another of the trio, its favored recipient
incurred the envy and criticism of the neglected
two.

"I come along by the buck-pen to-day," remarked the Deacon to the Cook, in one of those
outbursts of confidence which were rare with
him, "and there I seen somethin' thet done me
good. You know how musical the Oracle hez
been lately. Well, he was a-singin' thet duet
of Miss Kate's from the 'Muskrat' or somethin'
or other, an' a-blatin' to her about how much
he liked herdin' sheep, and she was a-replyin'
very sweet about how particular fond she was
of tendin' turkeys, and all the while thet
McCarthy buck was a sort o' sniffin' the air and
pawin' a little, ez ef he reckoned it disturbed
his peace of mind; and then, when they got
down to thet wind-up, where they were givin'
their imitations of the critters they admire, I
seen him put his head down and step back a
few paces, an' I knowed what was comin'.
Well, my boy, I'm a tenderfoot ef he didn't
take the Oracle plum aft just when he was

a-reachin' fur high C, and lifted him clean over three sheep. I nearly broke my heart laughin'."

Although the merriment of both Cook and Deacon seemed to argue that both regarded the Oracle's mishap as a species of retribution for an unwarrantable monopoly of the young lady's attractions, yet my duty as a veracious chronicler compels me to state, that the Deacon eventually consulted the Oracle in reference to certain conversations which the Cook was wont to hold with this coveted Miss, while he was occupied in the prosaic employment of washing dishes, and that it was a matter of grief to each —as an unconscious index of preferment—that on one occasion the condescending goddess had actually assisted him in this menial occupation. Similarly, when the Deacon developed a tendency to cull fresh wild-flowers morning after morning, and to place them in a vase as a votive offering to the fair one, the opinion prevailed with both masculine critics that he was altogether too bold and officious.

But the tendency to disunion on the part of the partners was speedily checked by a circumstance that called for a concentration of forces.

A visit to the neighboring sheep-pen in the gray dawn—one week after the arrival of the disquieting element—revealed the fact that their flock had been increased by forty new arrivals during the previous night. These callow innocents were shivering in the early morning air, and with plaintive bleats accepting the misery of infancy in all the despondency that young lambs exhibit. Their worthy mothers—evidently bewildered by the similarity of their various progeny—were in the customary agonies of doubt as to which one of the awkward unfortunates was her particular property. One and all, however, exhibited that proud elevation of the head and intractable obstinacy which only the maternal ewe can successfully affect, and with which she invariably sees fit to signalize her acceptance of the higher responsibilities of life.

In short, from calm, methodical sheep they had been transformed into anxious, nervous, and panic-stricken mothers, and were clamorous for assistance in their emergencies. All was complaint and confusion. Here two stubborn ewes had resolved to contest the ownership of one grotesque infant, and it needed the sagacity of King Solomon to detect the impostor, while the poor foundling of the recreant ran helplessly hither and yon, meeting the scorn and rebuffs of all respectable sheep. Here, a good mother divided her affections over a pair of pretty twins, and there, bereavement was attended with loud lamentation, and in a remote corner of the pen " Rachel, mourning for her children, refused to be comforted."

Apparently the Arcadian life of a sheep-ranch was at an end, and more serious labors awaited these Strephons of the frontier. Something of the sternness of this conviction was upon them, as the partners threw aside their coats and sprang into the pens. Then, indeed, was displayed the superior intelligence of man. The young lambs and their mothers were all "cut out" carefully from the main herd, and segregated in one of the small pens; while the bleating flock poured from the brush barriers, and went forth under the care of dog and herder for the pasturage of the day. One of the twins was "blanketed" with the hide of the dead lambkin and placed in a crib with the lamenting mother, until such time as she decided to accept it as the offspring she had lost. Such ewes as were dis-

posed to ignore **the claims** of parentage **were**
tethered to various trees, and **their** lambs placed
beside them, **that in** the solitude of their companionship they might be taught to forget their
idiosyncrasies. So that it was upon a busy and
bustling camp that Miss Kate dawned later—
an immaculate vision **of** starched serenity—
dainty-cuffed, snowy-collared, **and** with **an**
amused curiosity **in** her brilliant eyes.

And here she was made acquainted with **her**
own share in their labors, for the **Old** Man **had**
decided that she must **pay the penalty** of **her**
visit by taking charge **of the** buck-herd from
day to **day. In vain his** younger associates
protested, and advised that the young lady
should have company ; their gallantry **was un-**
availing **against the deductions** of the Old
Man's logic.

And so it happened that, an hour later, **an**
erect and graceful shepherdess, equipped
against the admiration of the ardent sun with a
gaudy parasol, and additionally **armed** with **a**
fantastic crook, **fared out upon the prairie with**
the solemn husbands **of the flock.** I wot their
ovine majesties **were** entirely unaccustomed to
the tutelage of so charming a Bo-peep, but their

grave deportment betrayed nothing of the charm of novelty. They appeared to accept Miss Kate as an unnecessary, albeit a very picturesque fact ; and, after they had thrown her into "unpicturesque hysterics," by an apparent disagreement as to whether their route lay up or down creek, and which they proposed to decide by a reverberating cannonade against one another's skulls, they were as serious in demeanor, and as pre-occupied with their own affairs, as these discreet and masculine sheep are wont to be. So that when the young lady had tired of noting their general resemblance to a lot of old hook-nosed Rabbis, the novelty of tending them began to pall, and she was driven first to her book, and eventually to gathering wild-flowers, from an absolute dearth of any appreciative object to exercise feminine arts upon.

And here she exhibited the customary nervousness of a sensitive and discriminating sex, for at every turn Miss Kate was apparently fearful of hidden terrors, with which her feminine imagination peopled the surrounding wilds, and every rustle of the short prairie grass was deprecated with certain shivers and forced retreats—presumably apprehensive of those "horrid snakes" which, since the misfortune of Mother Eve, have been so terrifying to her many daughters. When, therefore, she had thankfully escaped the bristling horror of an inoffensive horned-toad, that skittered* tremulously away at her approach, she was obliged to run the gauntlet of a brilliant lizard—actually two and one-half inches in length—that regarded her with glittering eyes and palpitating throat from an adjacent stone, and two chattering prairie-dogs, which appeared to resent the gaudiness of the young lady's parasol. And so it came to pass that Miss Kate, with this parasol advanced like a shield, and her crook poised and aggressive—a rosy, but defiant Amazon, very much out of breath, and with one of her dark tresses escaping from her hat and dancing upon her shoulder—encountered an animal more dangerous than any she had yet met, but one with

---

* The "horned toad" of Texas has, in a state of health, a quick, darting movement. Such specimens as we see here are usually half or entirely starved, and have no vitality. They *never* hop.

which she was far better qualified by bounteous nature to contend.

For there, recumbent and solitary in a little grassy hollow, was the Oracle, gazing vacantly up into the blue sky, where a gray hawk—a mere soaring speck in the limitless ether—was wheeling slowly heavenward. Undoubtedly Miss Kate recoiled with a little scream of astonishment, and expressed her great surprise at finding him thus idle when his associates were so busy at the ranch; whereupon it appeared that the Oracle had been in quest of the horses, as was his daily habit, and, being somehow unable to find them, had thrown himself down to rest a few moments before proceeding further. Accordingly, when this careful maiden had accounted satisfactorily for the present whereabouts of the young man, she became entirely oblivious of the necessity of future movement on his part, and sitting down beside him, challenged him with feminine inconsistency to an Arcadian *tête-à-tête*, in the course of which she expressed herself with a surprising wealth of superlative as completely carried away by the poetry of the ranching life. And then it appeared how different was the

Oracle's view; how he had had five years of this tedious experience, and was heartily sick and tired of it; how he was alone in the world and destitute of sympathy—at which point Miss Kate being rash enough to offer hers, she was immediately informed, with all the ardor of a Southern temperament, that it lay in her power to dissipate all this misery and to make the Oracle the happiest of men.

It is my duty to state at this juncture that when Miss Kate was thus confronted with the havoc her charms had wrought, she was seized with contrition, and experienced that remorse which her sex are unaccustomed to develop until too late for practical purposes. Yet I can not entirely exonerate her from all blame.

A lady of her attractions, and who had been accustomed to note the demoralizing tendencies of her arts whenever she chose to smile upon the masculine portion of frontier society, should certainly have refrained from exerting her fascinations upon the inexperienced ranchman. Now that the mischief was done, she impressed upon the Oracle as kindly as she could the impossibility of his request, and then was suddenly overwhelmed with grave misgivings for the welfare of her neglected sheep, and left the discomfited gentleman quite abruptly. But once out of his presence, the regretful beauty was overcome by a surprising gayety and by fits of uncontrollable laughter which she was fain to explain at intervals throughout the afternoon in bursts of confidence to her indifferent flock.

With few interruptions and extraordinary success the labors of the ranchmen of Concho County were prosecuted. It is with pleásure that I record, as an instance of the refining power of woman, that these labors were unaccompanied by the customary profanity. It will be perhaps difficult for me to impress my civilized reader with the edifying quality of that morality which could resist the temptations of the time. They have not known the trials and perplexities of the lambing season. But when I assure them that it is customary for sheepmen to compress within these short six weeks the entire profanity of the year, and testify that during this privileged season I have myself detected grave elders of the Church, and even frontier gentlemen of the clerical profession, voicing their wrath in opprobrious epithets, and hurling lurid contumely upon certain refractory ewes, I trust I may convey some slight notion of the phenomenal character of their forbearance. Yet even in this blameless fashion days and weeks flew by, and Miss Kate's visit was drawing to a close.

It was then that our lovely Urania became disagreeably conscious that the Cook had exchanged his functions for those of a sighing Strephon. His customary loquacity was gone; his culinary efforts were mechanical and unsuccessful; the bacon was invariably burned and the bread inexcusably sour. Given over to "flashes of silence," he was moody and distraught.

Personally experienced in noting the ravages of the tender passion in the sterner sex, Miss Kate viewed the emergency with manifest foreboding, and endeavored to avert the impending crisis by avoiding him, and showing a marked preference for the society of the reserved and diffident Deacon. It chanced, however, that on a certain rainy day the lady found it necessary to seek the cheering warmth of the kitchen fire, and there, after a long and depressing silence, the Cook, who was engaged in setting

the table, asked her, in a sadly despondent
tone, if she had ever noticed how lonely a
knife looked without a fork being placed beside
it. Miss Kate, with a boding feeling of alarm,
was coldly unconscious of this characteristic of
cutlery.

"I reckon it's just thet way I look, for it's
certainly the way I feel, Miss Kate," said he,
"when you're away with them sheep on the
range. A month ago I wouldn't have thought
it possible, but now, unless I can get a glimpse
of your purty face, I'm as soggy as bread without 'east, and as flat as beans without salt.
Lookin' at it by an' large, I reckoned the best
thing for me to do was to jest naturally state
the case to you, for, if you've no objection to
pull in double-harness—why—one-quarter of
them sheep's mine, and we'll start a ranch to-
morrow on our own account." He raised his
eyes, which had been cast down embarrassedly,
but Miss Kate had ungraciously fled, leaving
him staring with the knife-box in his hand.

The lady absented herself from dinner that
day on the plea of lack of appetite, but in the
seclusion of her little room was visited by the
same unaccountable merriment that had seized
her on another occasion.

Late that night, as Miss Kate was about to retire, she discovered an uncommonly large bouquet upon her little table, and a small slip of paper protruding from the petals of a flaming cactus that seemed to her apprehensive fancy to typify the ardent devotion of the sender. Hurriedly seizing this she read the following letter, which, from the many blots that covered it, and the painfully cramped nature of the handwriting, suggested great labor as well as embarrassment in its composition :

"SWEETEST MISS—I've been puttin off speakin to you about suthin thet hez botherd me fur a right smart chance, an somehow I never cud git to say it to you yet. I spoke to the old man about you yesterday and he like to kill himself alaughin, so I didnt quite make him out, but reckon it tickled him. I sorter suspicioned youd ketch on from the bokays—for I wouldnt botherd so much fur eny other gal an I reckon yer the peartest in all Concho an ye seem to be tuk with sheep-ranchin so I reckon ye know what I mean now an if your agreeable please ware thet purple dress an thet big white collar that makes you look just like an angell, an I am yours.   DEACON."

It is needless to say that the young lady appeared to be afflicted with mental obliquity in regard to the meaning of this vague epistle, but, as a precautionary measure, appeared in an entirely different dress at breakfast the following day.

It was toward sundown, several days after this, that Miss Kate—as demure *now* as she was pretty—requested her three suitors to accompany her to the top of a neighboring "divide," whither she had of late been wont to repair, and from which the road to Paint Rock was plainly visible. As they toiled up the ascent her manner was eager and her face flushed and expectant. Soon after their arrival they perceived a horseman approaching them at a gallop. As he drew near it was apparent, from the unmistakable clothes of his calling, that he was a handsome cow-man, evidently returning from some remote "round-up." After the fashion of those knights of the rein, he did not check his speed until almost upon them, when his skilled hand threw his mustang upon his haunches, and, dismounting, he approached them rather mysteriously from out the cloud of dust that hung above the fury of his sudden halt. But the three partners were shocked to see *Miss* Kate throw herself with a cry of joy into the arms of this gallant equestrian, and completely stunned by her instantly presenting him to the trio as her absent husband. In a surprisingly short space of time the reunited couple were left alone upon the hill.

But, half-way down the descent, the Oracle stopped and laid a hand upon the rugged shoulder of each of his companions, and gazed into their humiliated eyes.

"To think, boys—to think—thet for the last six weeks thet ornery Old Man has been takin' on in private, and quietly playin' this hull out-fit—*thet's what jest naturally gets me!*"

AN EPISODE OF PAINT ROCK.

——o——

IT was the close of the Spring "round-ups." For weeks past the hollow valleys had resounded with angry bellow and hurrying hoof. The organized bands of horsemen that with goading shout and swinging lariat had pressed the flying squadrons of the plains were all disbanding and breaking up. The last calf had been roped and branded ; the last drifting estray cut out and turned back into his own territory. Left to themselves at last, the tortured, panic-stricken cattle dispersed in straggling troops along the river-bottoms, or panting sought the shade and security of the higher hills.

It was indirectly due to this fact that the little town of Paint Rock, on the afternoon of May 5, 1883, was the scene of exceptional hilarity. Not that its usually quiet and

well-behaved inhabitants took part or shared at
all in the present excitement.   A long contemplated picnic had absorbed its feminine attractions, and apparently levied largely upon its
masculine resources.   The present levity was to
be attributed entirely to the irruption of a discordant and unusual element.   For the past
fortnight stray bands of cow-boys had been
dropping into the little frontier town, until on
the afternoon in question its single narrow
street was unpleasantly vocal with these
knights of the rein.   It would seem that the
available remainder of its citizens was needed
to represent the two prominent business interests of the locality.   Within the popular precincts of his seductive saloon, Mr. James Wily
dispensed alcoholic consolation over his narrow
bar, and held out the fascinations of civilization
in the musical click of billiard balls and the
ominous rattle of other ivory that was not
spheroidal.

" Yer see how it is," explained " Kickapoo
Dick," to the unsuspecting spouse whom he had
lately wedded, and who had discovered certain
parti-colored discs in the pocket of his ducking
jacket,—" When a feller plays a game of bil-

lards, he hez the privilege o' takin' a drink or gettin' a check. Now *I* allers takes a check."

At the upper end of the village the rival establishment of Hackett's furnishing store, apparently possessed an equal attraction in the prominent display of revolvers, leathern leggings, knee-boots, sombreros, " slickers," and other frontier articles of utility and adornment. Both did a flourishing business, and their incoherent and effusive patrons—in the expressive vernacular of Paint Rock,—were engaged in " *running the town.*"

Doubtless this peculiar enterprise of the Texan cow-boy possessed little interest for Mr. Josh Blunt. He had officiated at too many performances of like nature to find their details either novel or engrossing. When, therefore, the eccentric gentlemen in the billiard-saloon evinced a disposition to begin the festivities with a wild and grotesque war-dance, accompanied by an opening overture of six-shooters discharged at different points of the compass, but chiefly, with a becoming disregard for other occupants of the premises, into the ceiling overhead, he languidly detached either elbow from the bar—in which attitude he had been absorbed in throwing dice—and quietly **passed** from the room.   Neither did the equestrian accomplishments of several of his brethren **who** were engaged in the ostentatious breaking of a wild mustang engross his attention, and he beheld one of them ride the pony up a flight of steps **and** into the main room **of a** furnished **house with the** same pensive unconcern.

Apparently in search of excitement, **he** strolled listlessly through the village, and **eventually** into the store of Hackett.   Here **he** gravely resisted the hospitality of **a** large paint-sign which the enterprising proprietor had hung out in generous rivalry of the lower establish**ment,** and whose flaming capitals had hitherto engrossed the immediate attention of all callers. **"** *Whisky Free in the Back Room* **"** was the **purport** of this popular announcement.   Here, with the same imperturbable gravity, he beheld **Rube** Smart purchasing a one-hundred-dollar saddle, and strapping it carefully upon a lean, broken-winded *broncho* of the value of twenty-**five** ; others exhibiting the customary solicitude in the purchase **of expensive** hats and boots, and displaying a corresponding contempt for cloth**ing** intermediate parts of **the** body ; and noted variously, with the sneer of a superior philosophy, that unpardonable extravagance which, in the American cow-boy, is the inevitable accompaniment of excessive stimulation. And here he received an answer to a note which he had dispatched earlier in the afternoon, the receipt of which caused him to look graver than ever.

The fact was, the expectations of Mr. Josh Blunt had just been severely dashed. He had confidently set aside this particular afternoon for a long meditated call upon Miss Flo Brooks, a local belle. With due deference to the demands of Texan etiquette, and in entire accordance with the established precedents of frontier society, he had given notice of his purpose by a preliminary note. I think that Mr. Josh Blunt was dimly aware that the terms in which he couched his intention were not particularly happy. That, as he laid down his pen, he was struck by the resemblance borne by his rude handwriting to an erratic assortment of cow-brands, I am quite positive. However, a consciousness of the fact that his former essays in chirography had been limited to the branding of his cattle and camp equipments with his

characteristic label 3. X. C., and that his im-
plements had been respectively a hot iron and
a jack-knife, may have made his own criticism
of his efforts peculiarly generous and charitable.
"C. U. BY. 3." was the terse and somewhat
rebus-like expression of Mr. Blunt's laconics.

But however legible had been the announcement of the gentleman's purpose, its import
was apparently unavailing. The message was
returned with the information that Miss Brooks
was not at home that afternoon, and Mr. Blunt
was correspondingly chagrined and disconsolate.
Who had the boy seen? Only Old Man Brooks,
who was setting out trees in his door-yard. Did
he know definitely where Miss Flo had gone?
No! Old Brooks definitely didn't; all he could
say was that Miss Flo had disappeared immediately after dinner, and as her pony was gone
from the barn, he "reckoned she'd took a ride
somewhar." Mr. Blunt must call again.

Accustomed to note the freedom that characterized Miss Brooks's movements, Mr. Blunt did
not feel called upon to express himself in regard
to Old Brooks's ignorance of his daughter's
whereabouts, or to advert disparagingly upon
his many short-comings as a parent. In com-

mon with the rest of the eligible youth of the locality, Mr. Blunt had long ago arrived at the conclusion that if Old Brooks attempted any innovations in parental government, or any infringements of personal liberty, he would have his hands full in enforcing them. Miss Flo was known to have a mind of her own, and to be tenacious of keeping it. The wife of Old Brooks—a faded " specimen of Texan efflorescence "—after a few vain attempts in the way of suggestion and precept, had resigned in despair. Left to the inadequate care of her father, she was accredited with the distinguishing accomplishment of " running the old man."

Perhaps she had very little to run. Old Brooks was a cheerful example of thriftless good fortune. As an instance of the pecuniary reward that awaits persistent endeavor, he was not a success. He was a native of the State, and in his early life had accepted the easy, shiftless, vagabond life of a frontier tramp. He had bloomed and blossomed with the prairie grasses, and apparently with as little effort. An overweening confidence in the enticements of " Mexican Monte " absorbed his scanty earnings,

and the acceptance of Paint Rock whisky as a
fortifier against pecuniary loss had at one
time threatened to abbreviate his "gilded and
ephemeral existence." But a day of triumph
dawned. In one short hour of marvelous
luck, Brooks absorbed the capital and broke
the bank of the " Blue Goose Saloon." I have
not space to dilate upon the round of fashionable dissipation with which Brooks saw fit to
signalize his phenomenal good fortune. Suffice
it that at the end of a week—most of the inhabitants of Paint Rock being in consequence
in a state of depressed alcoholism—he awoke
to a consciousness of disorganized nerves, and
the decease of the ruined gambler who had
sought surcease of sorrow in suicide. In a fit
of remorse Brooks buried the professional
gentleman, and invested the sum left from his
convivial exploits in a herd of cattle. If, in
accordance with natural laws, this investment
had quadrupled in value, Brooks had little
more than impulse to thank for his present
wealth. But with the assumption of social im-
portance and position as a cattle owner, he discarded his dissipated habits. Not so for a long
period, his primitive method of housekeeping,

or his frontier style of dress. It had not occurred to Brooks that bacon and beans as an article of diet, or rawhide and red-flannel as an external covering, were inconsistent with his rank as the richest cattle man in Concho County. He received his first intimations on this head from his aging wife and maturing daughter. Acting by an inspiration from that quarter, he had erected a commodious frame house, furnished it sumptuously, and somewhat suspiciously accepted some of the comforts of a growing civilization; but he still resisted all attacks upon his conventional raiment as an infringement of an inherent prerogative. This singular obstinacy was a matter of deep grief to the shoddy sensibilities of Mrs. Brooks.

"Yer jest blightin' Flora's prospects and killin' the rest of the furniture by yer ornery an' permiskiss appearance," she had remarked to him on one occasion. As the catalogue of Miss Flo's suitors had hitherto included only illiterate cow-men, Mrs. Brooks's remonstrance seemed scarcely pertinent. Indeed, the aspiring tendencies of mother and daughter had obtained for them the distinction of being "stuck-up." This social attitude was visited with appropriate resentment by their female neighbors.

"Ef thet woman o' Old Brooks allows to lord it over me by slingin' style," said Mrs. Judge Treddle, as she stretched a temporary clothes-line between the posts of her front-gallery,—"I reckon I'll remind her o' what she was onct. 'Pears she's clean forgot that she an' me took in washin' when this yer town was only a camp. An' the airs o' thet Flo o' her'n, with her starched petticoats and embroidered flounces, a reckonin' herself a heap better nor my Clorinder, along o' her Galveston eddication, an' novel readin', and sendin' out her duds to git washed! I ain't naterally no patience with her for a lazy, stuck-up piece!"

Whereupon the indignant matron, with much exaggeration of effort and appropriate derisive pantomime, exhibited herself at the washtub to the gaze of her former laundry assistant, when she took her customary afternoon ride, and hung up her entire contribution to that lady's fading memory, in flapping and humiliating testimony upon the front porch.

All these peculiarities of his Dulcinea's family were familiar to Mr. Josh Blunt, as he accepted his disappointment, and lounged slowly back to the Blue Goose Saloon. All at once it occurred to him that he would have an early opportunity of meeting his fair one. He was reminded first of an impending "hop" at the residence of Old Brooks, and second of his degraded corporal condition. It occurred to him that his appearance might be improved and his feelings benefited by the luxury of a bath. He was so impressed by this reflection that he communicated it to the gentlemanly proprietor of the Blue Goose.

"My Christian friend," said that gentleman, walking to the doorway, and comprehending Blunt's unwashed exterior and the remote landscape in a single glance of paternal solicitude, "yonder is the Concho River, and here's a piece of soap! Perhaps from gin'ral appearances it might improve you to take advantage of both. Far be it from me to prevent any hankerin' o' yours for thet kind of refreshment, but I keeps no bathin' establishment!"

With which cheerful avowal he resumed his duties at the bar, and the astonished Mr. Blunt leaped into his saddle and galloped away.

Meanwhile, the missing Camilla of his affec-

tions, mounted upon her little pony, was scour-
ing the long levels that led to the Ford, very
picturesque in her pretty riding-dress, very
animated in demeanor, and very rosy with
exercise.   An hour before the arrival of Mr.
Blunt's missive she had slipped quietly to the
barn in the rear of her father's house, and
"cinching" the saddle-girths of "Pansy" with
her own pretty, trembling fingers, dashed away
over the trackless prairie with a careless freedom that betrayed her familiarity with her
surroundings.   Indeed, in an æsthetic sense, it
was a matter of regret that there was no appreciative spectator to carry away with him the
memory of her charming presence.   From the
wild verbenas which an inspiration peculiarly
feminine had led her to twine among the dark
tresses of her imperious little head, to the
shapely, well-booted foot that peeped occasion-
ally from the plunging skirts of her habit, she
was very bewildering in a locality where that
epithet could not with safety be applied to the
majority of her sex.   But if she escaped the
admiration of a society perhaps too extravagant in its appreciation of feminine charms,
there were other animate critics unusually

voluble. It seemed to Miss Flo that she had never known the prairie-dogs so enthusiastic, applauding her in pigmy hosts, with monotonous encore, from their many burrows, or sitting speechless, bolt upright, and with protesting fore-paws acknowledging her many fascinations. A monkish chaparral-bird who was out that afternoon on his regular parochial calls was constrained to mount the trunk of a fallen tree and survey her admiringly as she passed. After which he hurried away, shaking his grave head beneath its cowl, as if he were more than usually impressed with the vanity of all earthly things. And even when she neared the river, a heavy, lumbering owl, slipping from the shady depths of a pecan, was fain to express his surprise in a soft "Hoo-oo!" of inquiry—a question which he had never, hitherto, felt called upon to ask by daylight.

I think Miss Flo was glad to reach her rendezvous. Certainly her manner was eager, although about her moist, red lips there was a playful petulance that was, perhaps, as dangerous as it was fascinating. The spot where she had halted was singularly picturesque and charming. It was a little hollow in the river's margin,

embowered among the mesquites whose scanty
shade was supplemented by clinging creepers
and trailing vines.   Within its leafy circle a
jubilant spring—that brawled over a ledge of
rocks, and dripped its crystal overflow into a
rocky basin—held out a promise of coolness
and quiet amid a flickering half-light of spray
and shadow, particularly grateful after the fierce
glare without.   Through a rift in the foliage,
the broad, sluggish Concho glistened in the
sunlight, and sparkled away in slow moving
shallows, over which a fish-hawk, intent upon his
finny prey, was tremulously poised.   And away
on the farther bank, a motte of huge pecans,
standing like giant sentinels over the dwarfed
landscape, filled the eye with remote vistas in
their shady, twilight aisles.

It was very still.   Sitting quietly in her
saddle, Miss Flo could hear distinctly the shout
of some of the picnickers on the farther shore,
and even catch a glimpse of a fluttering ribbon,
or the gathered skirts of some curious rambler
against the painted bluffs beyond, still picturesque with the uncouth record of a fleeting
race.

Indeed the little frontier village had its

memories of the warlike Apaches. But their
familiar frescoes had little interest for the fair
equestrienne.

Her quick eyes wandered rapidly and dis-
appointedly up and down the river. Then she
turned them listlessly upon objects within her
bower. Here they encountered other hiero-
glyphics—equally rude, but modern in character.
From the nature of these sculptured legends,
this sequestered spot seemed to suggest a tryst.
There was the likeness of a rude heart upon
the opposite tree; grievously transfixed by the
archery of Cupid. And lower down were
certain letters and initials, united by the curving
brace with which youthful sentimentalists are
wont to indicate mutual affinity.

Suddenly a plaintive murmur was wafted
from the opposite shore. Miss Flo raised her
head with a slight start. The dim spaces of
the remote pecans were filled with white, tum-
bling, flocculent masses that surged against their
trunks, and ran nervously along the river's
margin. A rising flush crimsoned her tell-tale
cheeks, and half unconsciously she murmured
the single word—" Sheep ! "

The shrinking, timid herd recoiled from the

brink, exhibiting a feminine coyness about wetting their dainty buskins. At last a horse-man made his way slowly through the dividing throng, leading by a confining rope a reluctant ewe whose bell tinkled fitfully as if in remon-strance and alarm. Still seated in the saddle, he plunged into the shallows, dragging behind him his timorous charge. A wail of deprecation rose from the woolly spectators upon the shore. Then they developed a solicitude and sympathy peculiarly ovine, running anxiously from point to point, and impatiently chiding the receding captor. A few of the boldest ventured into the pebbly shoals; their example was instantly followed by others who thronged behind them. And first a trembling, swaying, pontoon-like barrier was stretched across the silent river; and then an irregular, surging host, deprecating the discomforts of this enforced paddling.

Hidden within her leafy covert that concealed her brilliant eyes and heightened color, Miss Brooks scrutinized carefully the approaching horseman. He appeared to be a strong, well-made Englishman, with a good-humored face that had lost something of its ruddy complexion before the fierce sun of southern latitudes. Not

until he had dismounted and was bending com-
passionately over the discomfited ewe which
seemed to have absorbed an unnecessary amount
of water in her enforced fording and was quite
faint and dripping, did the young lady betray
her presence. At this juncture she coughed
slightly and waved a small handkerchief. The
young man looked up, caught sight of the
fluttering signal, and, with an exclamation of
pleasure, sprang again into the saddle and rode
hurriedly into the bower.

I have a reluctance about transcribing the
particulars of the meeting that took place
within those sacred precincts. As a matter of
fact, however, a contemplative raven that was
lazily sunning himself in an adjacent tree-top,
had his finer feelings shocked by the informality
of the young lady's greeting, and the enthusiastic advances of her companion. There was a
certain novelty, too, about the proceedings, aris-
ing from the fact that the *tête-à-tête* was equestrian, and that there seemed to be an occult
sympathy between their mustangs, who pressed
their heaving flanks together, while their riders
leaned across in their saddles, and exchanged
certain salutes and caresses, that, to the mind

of the somber and solitary ascetic upon the limb above, appeared entirely inconsistent with confidential communication.   He croaked his disgust and flew away.

Then there were murmurs too, and hand pressures, preliminary to a not overwise conversation, but which, perhaps, the sincerity of expression pardoned.   In the course of which there were certain vague references to Galveston that probably accounted for this surprising intimacy, and the disclosure that a Mr. Percy Russell was just from Abilene with 2,000 head of California yearlings, and on his way to his newly purchased ranch upon Upper Kickapoo.   Incidental to all this, a little episode occurred, which—had the boding raven remained to see it—might have possibly disarmed his former scruples.

Having possessed himself of one of Miss Flo's small hands, he slipped a glittering circlet upon a dimpled finger with a light, caressing touch.   He was still holding these dimpled fingers in his own, when there was a sudden crash in the underbrush, the jingling of spurs, the snort of a hurrying steed, and a burly figure, surmounted by a swarthy, scowling face,

grasping the reins in his left hand, and a bar
of yellow soap in his right, burst abruptly into
the inclosure. He gave the surprised couple a
hurried, confused stare ; grew suddenly white ;
and dashed fiercely away before they had time
to change their position. Both uttered a
forced laugh and glanced embarrassedly at one
another. A silence followed, so long as to be
both painful and distressing.

The pathos of love's communion seemed to
have been dissipated by this rude interruption.
Miss Flo soon bethought her of returning home,
and Mr. Russell was reminded that his herds-
men were arriving with the stragglers and de-
linquents of his flock.

" Mind that you come to the 'hop' at the
house,—to-morrow night, dear!" was her parting injunction. "And dress just as you did at
the 'Assemblies' in Galveston," she added with
feminine impulse ; " I'm so sick of these frontier
costumes! "

Then there was a very pretty, momentary
tableau, during which Miss Flo's slightly aqui-
line profile was outlined against a manly bosom,
and then the hurrying footsteps of her horse
were heard in the distance.

Before noon of the next day there were
rumors in Paint Rock that an unpleasant encounter had taken place at the river. These
were necessarily vague, but sufficiently definite
to awaken lively anticipations in a community
where trifling social differences were often attended with sanguinary details. Mr. Josh
Blunt had returned from his bathing trip,
without the bar of soap, but with no visible
signs of an ameliorated condition ; and his
garments exhibited signs of suffering from
thorns that were probably but a mild prototype
of his more deeply lacerated feelings. Immediately upon his return he had plunged into
unusual convivial excess, and, when somewhat
maudlin, had indulged in certain sarcastic and
defiant reflections, in which the recurring
phrases of " bloody Britisher," " bleeding John
Bull," together with frequent reiteration of
the statement that an inordinate amount of
blood was necessary to efface the recollection
of some unpardonable wrong, seemed to argue
a speedy gratification of the curiosity of his
auditors. It was at this time that his intoxicated judgment led him to dictate an indignant
letter to Miss Brooks, through the intervention

of Kickapoo Dick as amanuensis—a profound conviction insinuating itself even through his spirituous disguise that the language of symbols was entirely inadequate to the emergency.

" It seems to pint as ef things might be lively up to Old Brooks's to-night," remarked that gentleman to Mr. Wily, as he recruited himself from his labors at his genial bar. " Josh hez been sharpenin' thet bowie of his'n in a pensive, sighin' sorter way, ever since he got back, yestiddy, and whisky don't seem to improve him none. He allows to hevin' a strong pussonal bias agin the English shrimp from Abilene thet bought my ranch. Reckon it'd pay you to make a short call."

It was a hot night. The cool Gulf breezes that at that season are wont to take long rambles inland, visiting the odorous prairie with a refreshing coolness which is the prevalent charm of a Texan night, preferring to linger that evening in the embrace of the booming coast. There was an ominous glow in the sky, and all along the Northern horizon were sudden flashes of light that, at times, burst upon the eye in twisted corselets of fire, and gleaming links of chain lightning. Such stars as were visible were feeble and furtive, save where the planet Mars blazed with an angry flush above the dark outline of the painted bluffs beyond.

Lights twinkled in the Blue Goose Saloon, where business was unusually brisk in view of the coming festivity, and where the obliging proprietor, in the easy freedom of shirt sleeves and tilted cigar, attended to the many wants of his customers. The violent ringing of the bell of room No. 8 interrupted his labors.

"John!" called Mr. Wily from behind the bar,—"see what that English snipe is yankin' his bell about!" The individual addressed disappeared up the narrow stairway.

"Well, what is it? Cocktails?" he inquired perfunctorily, when the man reappeared a few minutes later. "Cocktails!" retorted the man ruefully, "nary time! He allows thet it disagrees with him to hev the profile of former hoccupants starin' hat 'im from hoff the pillow —don't yer know! And thet ef he's goin' to sleep thar to-night, yer must change the pillowcase."

This fastidiousness raised a laugh in the barroom.

"Tell him to pin his hankercher onto the pillow, and thet we don't make no provision for tenderfoots," responded the proprietor cheerfully.

The man departed with the message. But a violent jingling of the bell again recalled him.

"Well—what now?" inquired Mr. Wily with an air of resignation.

"He's howlin' fur water now,—and—towels!" gasped his breathless servant.

"Humph! Ain't thar no window-curtain in No. 8?" inquired the puzzled landlord. "Is it possible he don't know thet thar's a tin basin down in the bar-room, an' other toylet articles allus provided for the guests o' this yer Hotel?" he added impatiently. "Git! you idgit! he's playin' yer!"

But there were other demands, rapid, vehement, and persistent, culminating in the request for a better light.

"Tell that gilt-edged son of a Juke," screamed the now infuriated proprietor,—"thet the electric light's out of order, the telephone's broke, and the telegraph operator is out, just now, on a little *pasear*, but if it'll gratify him,

we'll send to New York by the next steamer
for all the modern improvements! Ask him ef
he's aware thet he's in Texas, on the frontier,
and only three years behind the Ingins! Tell
him," he added with withering sarcasm,—"thet
sence he wants the airth for fifty cents, we'll
engage it as soon as we can get the refusal, and
while we're about it we'll hev it fried and sent
up to his room."

But his eloquence was stopped by the appearance of his exacting guest, enveloped in a long
English ulster that swept to his heels, and with
an opera hat surmounting his audacious head.

Mr. James Wily leaned against the bar for
support; his guests recoiled in dismay; and
Kickapoo Dick, with an assumption of exaggerated alarm, played for a moment nervously
with the handle of his revolver.

"Wal, dern my skin!" exclaimed the former
audibly as the faultless figure passed out,—
"thet black nail kag hat is what thet feller had
in that leather-case;—I packed it up to his
room very careful, reckonin' it might possibly
be his duelin' pistols."

The commodious mansion of Old Brooks
was brilliantly illuminated, and its smiling

proprietor, conspicuous in a recently purchased red-shirt, and with his ingenuous features shining from ablutions unusually thorough, received his guests in the front-hall with awkward and labored cordiality.

Prudent preparations for the coming festivity had been made. The Brussels carpet, imported at great expense from Galveston, had been taken up in the parlors, and the modern furniture carefully removed. "Jest to give the boys an opportunity to turn loose and sling their spurs a little," he confidentially explained to the first arrival. The mantel-shelves were occupied by a processional torch-light parade of tallow candles inserted in lager beer bottles, and the posts of the front gallery on which the folding doors of the ball-room opened, supported several parti-colored japanese lanterns. The village school-master presided at the melodeon, and the violinist, who had come forty miles that day with the up-stage from Menard, was seriously rosining his bow. The invited guests, affluent in white shirts and aggressive in equipment as regards the masculine portion, and timid, blushing, and overburdened with ribbons and sentiment in their feminine con-

tingent—but all exhibiting that awkward preoccupation which characterizes individuals to
whom social events are only an episode, were
dispersed about the room, or apparently glued
to its blank walls, when a flutter of excitement
was caused by the entrance of Miss Flo, very
simply and tastefully dressed in white, and
leaning on the arm of Percy Russell, who was
in full evening dress. Then the hum of conversation was hushed by the voice of Old
Brooks, who had advanced to the center of the
room.

"And now, boys, wade in, and don't stop to
consider shoe-leather," remarked that genial
host with informal hospitality,—"Every thing's
ready for ye. Thar's whisky and cigars in the
supper-room for them that wants 'em, and cards
and social convarse for them as don't dance.
Likewise a music-box on the settin' room table
that winds up and may amuse them ez hezn't
seen one of them nateral tune-grinders. I
trust ye'll all act ez though ye was to hum,
and jist naturally enjoy yourselves."

And even with this easy introduction, the
fiddle squeaked, the melodeon wheezed a sonorous accompaniment, and the festivities began.

It was a gala night in the history of Paint
Rock.   Whether owing to a social spirit
engendered by the opening speech of the genial
Brooks, or attributable to the more potent
influences of the supper-room, the mirth and
fun were soon fast and furious. Legs that in the
saddle were supple and elastic, but in the measures of the dance wofully uncompromising and
erratic, whirled in the waltz and chasséed in
the quadrille. A few scions of the plains, carried away by enthusiasm, undertook certain
ambitious steps and gambols which, regarded
as inspirations acquired from a study of the
habits of frolicsome calves, were faithful and
painstaking, but did not contribute to the grace
or decorum of the occasion.

The festivities were at their height, and the
dancers engaged in the performance of a frontier favorite, wherein the taste of both sexes
was displayed and an opportunity afforded of
"bowing to the wittiest, dancing with the prettiest, and swinging the one loved best," and the
fiddler, absorbed in the calling of his figures
and carried away by his own harmony, with
rapt eyeballs and the grimaces of the natural
performer, was executing solitary pirouettes on

his own account, to the demoralization of some of the audience, when there was a shout, a muttered imprecation, the sound of a fierce, momentary scuffle, and a man writhing fiercely in the grasp of another who brandished a gleaming bowie, struggled into the center of the room. It needed but a glance to distinguish Blunt and Russell. But the latter, how changed! His dress-coat torn, his immaculate linen rumpled and soiled, his face bloodless and convulsed by the desperation of effort with which he restrained the other from using the knife.

A dozen hands separated the combatants. The frightened guests gathered about the excited group. Then followed words of explanation and remonstrance, that ceased as Old Man Brooks addressed the belligerent couple in a tone of querulous disapproval.

"It's playin' it rather low down upon me an' my family, gentlemen," he began rather feebly. "Is this yer an Abilene shindig that ye must come cavortin' round with bowie-knives?" he inquired of Blunt with a sudden access of energy.

That individual vouchsafed no reply. His eyes glanced hurriedly past his interlocutor; lighted up with a baleful fire as they rested upon his late antagonist ; and remarking, "Six-shooters!—on sight!" he turned on his heel suddenly and left the ball-room.

The music rose again but the spirit of festivity was broken. A more exciting topic possessed the minds of all. Guests, collected in little groups, discussed the recent incident, and rumor flew from lip to lip. Not a few departed altogether.

In the crowded supper-room, Kickapoo Dick, seated luxuriously cigar in mouth, related the details of the late unpleasantness to a breathless circle.

"The facts is simple, boys," said that gentleman, rising above the trammels of grammar in the sincerity of his narration,—" Me an' Josh settin' here smokin', passin' the bottle, and chattin' keerless and free. In comes thet English shrimp thet bought my ranch an' lights a *segar* on his own account. Josh looks up, sees English shrimp, strikes an attitude and says—'*A garsong! dern me! Here, waiter, parse me them biscuits!*' English shrimp looks insulted and fetches him one with thet accordion hat o' his'n. Josh draws immejet an' reckons to pin him, an' the rest yer knows."

In a corner of the front gallery, where the waning light of a delirious moon filtered through the clinging tendrils of a Virginia creeper, a pale face and two white arms were raised appealingly to some one hidden in the shadow.

"I'm so frightened, dear!" said a soft voice. "What *will* you do?"

"I fear there is but one way out of it," came sadly from the shadow.

"You mean that you must fight?" asked the soft voice tremblingly.

"I do," was the quiet answer.

"Oh, Percy! Percy!" sobbed the voice despairingly, as a cloud drifted over the moon and the corner of the gallery was enveloped in darkness.

Long before daylight the next morning the little village of Paint Rock was astir. A consciousness of the fact that two of its visitors were to "look for one another" at daybreak, made the usually tranquil slumbers of its inhabitants disturbed and restless. When it was understood that this inquiring search was to be prosecuted in the long, tangled swale that stretched for half a mile at the foot of the bluffs which gave the town its name, there were early pilgrimages in that direction.

It was a gray and ghostly dawn. Pale mists, rising from the river, were caught in the spreading branches of the pecans, or drifted lazily across the line of cliffs, whose grotesque figures and diabolical devices, streaked with carmine and vermilion, stared in the truthful light of early morning. With the first rays of the sun voices were heard on opposite sides of the swale.

" Make sure work of him, Josh ! This foreign capital is ruinin' the country ! " remarked Kickapoo Dick as he pressed a pair of regulation " Colts " into the hands of his principal.

" Don't fret yourself," retorted the other coolly. " I'll take care o' all thet."

On the other side, Old Brooks was parting from Percy Russell with much warmth and feeling.

" How's yer narves, my boy ? " he inquired anxiously. " Won't ye irrigate before ye start in ? " producing a black bottle from the side pocket of his ducking jacket. " Wal, tastes differ," he soliloquized, as Russell refused the proffered liquor. " Perhaps yer better without it. Howsomever, I done all my early fightin' on this yer sort of inspiration," he

added, indulging in personal reminiscence.
" Keep straight across by the sun. Line him
ef ye can, boy, and shoot smart, for he's right
peart with a six-shooter, Josh is."

With this encouraging advice he stepped
aside, and the Englishman disappeared in the
thick shrubbery.

Hours passed. The serried lances of the sun
pierced the tangled thicket, but betrayed no
sign of life in its silent depths. Overhead
from the blue empyrean a pair of hawks called
shrilly to one another, and wove their soaring
circles. Perched on the jutting crags above,
and outlined against the horizon, the spectators
watched and waited in breathless expectation.
Bets were freely offered and taken on the result.
Six-shooters and silver watches, Mexican spurs
and ivory-handled bowies staked with a freedom inconsistent with the value usually put
upon those articles, indicated the absorbing
excitement. Slowly the hours dragged along.
The lengthened strain was beginning to tell on
the audience. What must be its effect upon the
participants ? At last the sun, towering at the
meridian, sent the shadows northward. " The
odds are even," was the general comment as
they shifted their positions,

What was that? A shot surely, but so far away it sounded like the mere popping of a cork. A faint wreath of smoke rose and drifted away far to the right.

The crowd upon the ledge brightened up and listened. Ten minutes passed. Then, there being no repetition, the excitement flagged. The more elevated positions were abandoned; pipes were lighted; some were playing cards. Slowly the sun sank and the shadows lengthened.

At length a shout from Kickapoo Dick dropped the cards from the players' fingers.

A figure, splashed with mud, torn with the thicket, was visible on the trail nearest the river. *It was the Englishman.*

With shouts and exclamations of surprise, the men hurried down the sides of the bluff eager for the news. What were the particulars? Had he killed him at the first fire? With astonishment they heard his reply. He had not seen Blunt since the night before.

Not seen him? Had he not heard that shot? Yes, he had heard the shot, and turned in its direction, but had seen nothing. His pistols were undischarged.

They waited until the next morning and then

began to search for him. They sought him all that day and the next, pushing their inquiry far into the night with lantern and torch. Not until a gathering flock of buzzards proved an infallible compass upon that emerald sea were their labors rewarded. Then, with no mark of blade or bullet, they found him seated with his back against a bowlder, but so swollen and ghastly in death as to be almost unrecognizable. His revolver, with one chamber discharged, was by his side.

"Rattlers!" said Kickapoo Dick, kicking the stubby carcass of a snake, the head of which had been neatly severed by a bullet.

A STAGE-COACH ENCHANTRESS.

———o———

SHE was certainly very charming. Amid all the discomforts and annoyances of our journey, I think we were unanimous upon that point. In fact we had grown to regard as the only pleasant feature of that long ride the time spent in little innocent gallantries toward our fair fellow-traveler by way of alleviating its tiresome monotony for her.

But our attentions were preferred as simply an expression of that reverence which a discriminating sex feels called upon to pay in the presence of a beautiful woman. For we had learned that she was looking for her husband, and our polite rivalry was therefore neither selfish nor personal.

So that when the Doctor loaned her his only copy of Byron to read, it was looked upon as a graceful and becoming tribute to her fas-

Reprinted by courtesy of Mrs. Frank Leslie.

cinations, and when the Judge anticipated us in extending the courtesy of his traveling shawl, he was regarded rather as one who cheerfully embraced the opportunity of adjusting its woolen folds to certain soft and seductive feminine curves, than as one who thereby suffered any personal inconvenience.

After the handsome gentleman in black, with the luxuriant corn-colored beard, had barked his finger slightly in a gallant attempt to adjust a refractory window in the stage door, her tender solicitude and soft, feminine sympathy pervaded the coach with so extravagant a sentiment that I think she might have called upon the company collectively for the shedding of unlimited blood in her behalf, and unquestionably found it forthcoming.

We had been staging it since early morning between Belton and Lampasas, and had barely progressed more than half way. The vehicle in which we traveled had the generic quality, that is, it was frowsy, dingy and ill-conditioned, with something of the " dreariness of premature decay superadded."

It had the average number of decrepit springs below, that squeaked and protested, and the customary quota of leathern straps above, that swayed and beckoned in a spectral fashion amid the half-light of the dim interior, as we bumped, and jounced, and jolted on our way.

The roads had been heavy, and had discharged us at regular intervals from our seats inside, to plod and flounder onward beside the laboring conveyance—a wretched crew of grumbling pedestrians, under whose weary feet the mud rolled up and accumulated, until, to those compelled to carry this reluctant freight, they seemed to divide between them the entire soil of the State.

There is nothing which in quality can compare with Texan mud. It is a thing *sui generis.* It appears to be a compound of clay, india-rubber, molasses, and glue. It exhausts the impassioned rhetoric of the exasperated wayfarer, and inspires the hardened teamster with possibilities in profanity of which he has never dreamed.

" Nothin' but swarin' got me outer them ruts onct," said " Belton Joe," the driver, as he punched the black mud that had accumulated between the spokes, with a long cart-rung—

"nothin' but out an' out swarin', sure! The
coach was stuck; my whip was wore down ter
the stock; the off mare hed broke a trace; and
thet thar leader, 'Snipe,' was layin' down in the
harness, when I jes' rared up and invented a
cuss thet brought every thin' up stiff and standin'.
I may say," he added, reflectively, as he bit
off a triangular quarter of a large plug of tobacco
—"I may say I *histed* 'em out by sheer con-
densed cussin'. Perhaps now some on ye might
like to hear what I sed?"

But as the difficulties of the journey had already stimulated Joe to an ambitious display
of acknowledged powers in that direction, there
was an apparent reluctance on the part of his
auditors to any further rehearsal.

Perhaps our fair passenger appreciated our
feelings, and had a feminine intuition that her
presence alone restrained us from a hearty attempt to emulate the driver. Howbeit, at this
juncture her lovely head appeared at the window, and, with a gracious nod and smile, she
said:

"I imagine, gentlemen, by this time you
agree with General Phil."

"Why, what about General Phil?" inquired

the Doctor, as he kicked a discouraging mud-boat against the spokes of the wheel.

"What! Haven't you heard what General Phil Sheridan said, after a month of deploying cannon down in the Southern country?"

All were ignorant.

"Why, *he* said, gentlemen," replied the fair face, after a moment of delicious indecision— "*he* said, 'If he owned Hell and Texas, he'd live in Hell and rent out Texas.'"

Of course we were all a little shocked at this, but our laughter was none the less uproarious.

"Gad!" exclaimed an effusive passenger to the Judge, as he loitered behind to conceal his astonishment. "Isn't she a June-bug?"

"Young man," said the Judge, severely, stopping short in his tracks, and drawing up his portly figure to its full height, the more to impress his auditor—"young man, you should be ashamed—ashamed, sir, of giving utterance to that sentiment! The idea of your comparing woman—the loveliest conception of the Almighty, the sublimest creature that the Infinite Being has created, sir—to a disgusting bug, sir!"

The Judge, it should be said, who, as a former resident of the State of Kentucky, had a strong, chivalrous, and even romantic admiration for the sex, had himself fallen in the rear of the coach to recover his equanimity after the fair one's recent effort of memory.

However, when he had pensively gathered a few wild flowers by the roadside, including a flaming blossom of the prickly-pear, and had presented them to the lady with marked *empressement*, the incident was forgotten ; and when she had taken advantage of one of the long halts to ingratiate herself with the driver, and, climbing forward, so fascinated Belton Joe by a charming badinage of her own that he surrendered the reins temporarily into her keeping, we were all infected with the general infatuation.

The Judge, at this point, being entirely overcome, quoted Tennyson, and said so much about some one's "looking so lovely as she swayed the reins with dainty finger tips," and discoursed so eloquently upon the possibility of "wasting his whole heart in one kiss upon some one's perfect lips," that we grew apprehensive, fearing that even his legal lore might

not restrain him from an ambitious attempt to
play the part of Launcelot.

But after a few minutes more of wayfaring,
during which the road began obviously to mend,
we all returned to the coach, and I, yielding to
an overmastering impulse, assisted in restor-
ing the descending Guinevere to her former
position.

After this we proceeded once more in our
capacity of passengers, and regarded one another with the half-patient, half-bored expression of compulsory travelers.

Then some brilliant genius proposed playing
cards.

"Well, gentlemen," said the affable Doctor,
producing a pack from his portmanteau, "what
shall it be?"

"Euchre! I reckon," said the Judge, slyly,
after a long and careful scrutiny of the lady
from under his shaggy brows.

"Oh, dear, no," said the fair one, looking up
from her book and sitting up immediately.
"Now, don't say 'euchre' out of deference to
me. Why bless you! I know the men all hate
it, and I think 'poker' is twice as nice. Play
poker by all means; I always have the loveliest hands!"

A silence followed this audacious speech. How were we to interpret it? Were we to understand that she contemplated playing and intended thus to give us the hint? The embarrassment was general; the Doctor became absorbed in the gloomy landscape; the gentleman with the corn-colored beard nursed his recently injured finger with renewed solicitude.

At length the Judge mustered up courage, and said:

" But you know, my dear madam, we play a stiff game and give no quarter. It's only last night, at the hotel back in Belton, that my friend, the Doctor here, took sixty-eight dollars out of a single ' jack-pot.' "

This pecuniary statement apparently failed to strike terror into the fair passenger.

" Well," she retorted, with a charming smile, " can't you lower your ' ante ' a little, pray, on account of your company? You gentlemen are certainly unwilling to have it said that you kept a lady looking on by playing over her head."

Apparently this implied compliment to their gallantry carried conviction to the hearts of her masculine hearers, for the game was immediately made and proceeded without further comment.

It was not an interesting game. Owing to the jolting of the coach, and the fact that the cards were not a " poker-pack," there were afforded occasional stray glimpses of player's hands that deprived it of much of the possibilities of " bluff."

But I mention it, with the mortification of a sex that apparently regards proficiency in poker as a species of prerogative, that Victory, throughout that long December afternoon, was persistently a feminine goddess. Nor shall I soon forget the astonishment of the Doctor—a cool and skillful player—when, after raising his fair *vis-à-vis* to the extent of the limit, and finally throwing up four queens in a spirit of delicate courtesy, he discovered that his gallantry was forestalled by a quartet of aces.

Only once did an incident occur that in any sense alleviated our chagrin. This was when the effusive passenger, gathering up his cards eagerly after a fresh deal, unguardedly exclaimed that he would " bet his immortal soul " upon his present hand. Whereupon the lady, with great gravity, immediately "anted" a compensatory nickel and "called" him.

The players were recovering from the convulsions into which this ironical episode had thrown them, when there was a subdued exclamation from the driver, and all the available heads of the party were thrust from adjacent windows.

A magnificent buck had just crossed the road, and was tripping leisurely away through the scanty and dwarfed shrubbery. Revolvers were immediately produced by all hands, and a sharp and straggling fusillade followed at once from the windows of the coach, with the usual result among such pitiable marksmen, that their firing seemed to take the form of a running commentary upon the animal's capacity of speed, and was apparently so regarded by the deer, for he started, took a neighboring bush with inimitable grace, and was gone like a flash.

Our enthusiastic sportsmen now withdrew the protruding portions of their anatomy into the interior of the coach, apparently with the expectation of finding its female occupant in a dead faint but were correspondingly awed to find her erect and animated, peering at them eagerly through the blue wreaths of smoke and pungent odor of gunpowder that filled the vehicle, and inquiring eagerly whether the buck was down.

"Down!" echoed the Judge, with a rueful expression. "No, not exactly down; but hit hard, madam, *hit hard!* I saw him stagger sort of sideways just as I got it in on him with my last barrel, and the way he shook his 'flag' when he jumped thar, made me *know* I'd fetched him."

The effect of this shameless mendacity upon the feminine face before him was apparently not convincing. She smiled scornfully, and there was a marked superciliousness about her dainty eyelids.

"I don't believe any of you can half shoot," she finally exclaimed, with charming directness. "I'll wager now that I can beat you all."

Saying which, she produced from a pocket of her dress a small Derringer, and took aim at a little tree by the roadside.

The revolver cracked, and a splinter of bark flew from the sapling's side. The coach resounded with plaudits and bravos.

When this modern Diana had restored the weapon with a triumphant grace and heightened color, she settled back comfortably in her corner with an air of having said, " Now you see why I'm traveling alone, and that I'm perfectly competent to take care of myself,' closed her eyes dreamily, and actually went to sleep.

The coach jolted, the awed and observing men glanced at one another, the atmosphere of the dim interior seemed charged with re-pressed admiration.

For, as I have said at the outset, she was cer-tainly very charming. Albeit very plainly clad in a light-gray traveling dress, over which she wore a long, belted, brown ulster, her clear, cream complexion and brilliant color seemed to need none of the accessories of dress.

At present the saucy brown eyes, that had so inthralled her fellow-travelers, were veiled by the blue-veined lids whose jetty fringes swept her flushed little cheeks, and seemed to mourn over them quaintly.

Her red lips were parted slightly in slumber, and the short upper one curled like a dainty rose-leaf, exposing the brilliant little teeth that seemed to guard them.

I remember that, as I gazed at the flower-like mouth, I reflected with passing cynicism how "every rose has its thorn"; but when I noted how the wealth of her brown hair seemed to overburden the drooping, gracious head that swayed and nodded from side to side, I was ashamed of the reflection.

She had passed one plump and symmetrical arm through a strap that partially supported her against the jolt of the vehicle, and her two little feet, pushed resolutely out before her, and almost defiantly crossed, seemed to give her at once an air of courage and *abandon* that was not the least of her fascinations.

"Who's *that* she said she was lookin' for?" inquired the Judge in an awed whisper, turning upon us a face that ill concealed the admiration of a previous long and steadfast scrutiny.

"Her husband, I believe," replied the Doctor, with a very perceptible sigh.

"I wonder, gentlemen," musingly returned the legal representative of old Kentucky—"I wonder now, naturally, whether he's a *fighting* man."

"Ef he ain't," said the effusive gentleman,

whom the Judge had formerly rebuked for inelegant admiration—"ef he ain't, he isn't fit to have her, that's all."

Evidently his last remark was more popular than his previous comment, for the judge nodded approvingly.

Presently he expanded his chest with an air of authority, and looked around upon his auditors as if he were addressing a jury.

"Why, gentlemen," said he, in an emphatic *staccato*, "if it had pleased the Almighty to app'int me the terrestrial guar*deen* of that bewilderin' occupant of the back seat, it would have taken six yoke of Texan steers and a sheriff's posse to have got me away from her loveliness long enough to swear a witness— *long enough to swear a witness!* Yes, sir—by gad, sir."

Having thus demonstrated the superior claims of blooming womanhood to those of Texan jurisprudence, he relapsed into solemn silence.

But here there was a cynical chuckle from the front seat, and Belton Joe was observed to be laughing quietly to himself.

"What's that she's givin' ye?" he asked, abruptly, turning in his seat and looking in at the window.

"Who?" inquired the Judge, with some austerity.

"Party—back seat—inside," answered the driver, professionally.

"Says she's traveling—looking for her husband."

"Oh, yes!" responded the cynic. "Same game, I see."

"Do you know any thing of this lady?" inquired the Judge, solemnly.

"Wal," said Belton Joe, expectorating thoughtfully upon the axle as he reined up his laboring team, "ef hevin' her for a passenger for the last eighteen months, and no good comin' of it, is knowin' her, I reckon I does. Ef bein' able to swar my Bible oath ez to what her pertickler bizness is, ridin' on this yer road, I allow thet I don't. But it's allus the same old dodge. Allus lookin' for her husband; allus chipper as a jay-bird and sassy ez a chipmunk, with her shootin' off thet little 'Deranger'—and hittin' her mark, too, durn me!"

"Don't you reckon she's got any husband?" inquired the Judge, with growing interest.

"Wal, no," said Belton Joe, with a provoking wink; "I reckon I'm scarcely young enough to swaller thet jest yet. Some year ago, when I didn't know a brake from a whiffle-tree, or a leader from a wheel-hoss, p'r'aps yer might hev sugar-coated me to thet extent; but, hevin' hed some slight opportunity sence of lookin' at life by an' large, I reckon ye'll hev to excoose me."

"Well, what do you reckon, then?" said the Judge, impatiently, and apparently being in some haste to abandon the idea that the young lady was a species of frontier Evangeline.

"Wot do I reckon?" said Belton Joe. "Oh! I allows, in course, thet she's a widder—a widder with a taste fur travelin'—thet she's nat'rally keerless and free, an' thet her lettin' on to hevin' some feller she's tied to is a dodge to keep the men at a distance—thet's what I allows."

Saying which he whipped up his horses, and apparently discharged his mind of all further conjecture.

The coach sank again into the "monotonous cry of tired springs," and the creaking of complaining axles. Its occupants were apparently lost in reverie. The road was growing more lonely and the shadows were lengthening. The slant sunbeams of the declining sun shot through the window and sought me out upon the middle seat.

I retreated into the shadow. Here with my head reclining at ease, and the graceful swaying little figure before me, I abandoned myself to my own thoughts and fancies.

As a literary man and a regular contributor to the "Brady Bugle," I had encouraged and fostered my natural taste for romance, and my feelings on the present occasion partook of that quality.

Perhaps the pressing necessity for copy for the week's issue, precipitated my train of thought.

Howbeit, I found myself weaving a poetic wreath of associations and fancies about the unconscious figure over whose shapely curves the flecked sunlight danced and played. I was inclined to doubt the skeptical convictions of Belton Joe the more as the truthful influences of slumber relaxed and softened the bewitching features.

"Deception," said I, "lurking behind those

languishing eyelashes, dwelling upon those coral lips, or hiding in the dimples of those cheeks? Perish the thought!"

There is no telling at what conclusion I might have arrived; for, discarding all damaging reflections, I was drawing upon my imagination for facts, and making flattering forays in the "dim epistolary region of sentiment," when the sudden stoppage of the coach, and the sound of voices in altercation, suddenly recalled me to the present and the practical.

"Hands up, and tumble out here!" said a gruff voice.

At the same moment a pair of six-shooters were thrust in at the window.

"The first man that makes a motion or drops his hand *dies!*" the voice continued.

I started and looked up. A hard, resolute face, accenting the cold fires of two steel-gray eyes, was visible behind the cocked revolvers.

The passengers, to a man, accepted the resistless logic of the situation, and the fair inspirer of my recent dreams, being thus violently restored to consciousness, exhibited a surprising development of the imitative faculty of her sex.

Covered by the revolvers, which were held in dangerous proximity to our heads and increased our nervous haste—we speedily extricated ourselves from the coach.

Here, notwithstanding our trepidation, we perceived in the gathering twilight the figure of an accomplice stationed at a narrow point of the road a few rods in advance of the vehicle, evidently anticipating any stampede on the part of the driver.

" Form a line, with your hands up," continued our informal drill-sergeant, still disagreeably practical with his cocked revolvers.

In spite of the peril of our present position, there was something indescribably ludicrous in this marshaling of panic-stricken passengers into a compulsory awkward squad.

But the stern deductions of the situation followed too quickly to encourage merriment.

" Empty yer pockets of money and valuables ! " said our grim captor. " Look out for 'em now, Jack ! " he shouted sharply to his accomplice. " If they make a break, let 'em have it ! "

We silently obeyed, throwing down our worldly availables at the robber's feet with a reckless prodigality, and a suggestion of idolatry which might possibly have amused an observer not pecuniarily interested.

There was an irony of implied complicity in the bandit's methods that was peculiarly galling to the despoiled.

The ceremony was soon completed, this unsusceptible road agent even going so far as to accept a plump purse from the fair passenger, after which he added insult to injury by attempting to converse with her.

The innate chivalry of our party rebelled at this. We could stand being robbed, but this direct contempt for social etiquette was attended by immediate expressions of disapprobation.

In the same processional manner, and under the same unpleasant surveillance, we were escorted to our former seats, after which a gleam of fun lighted the stony eyes of the footpad, as he thanked us for submitting so gracefully, and, ironically doffing his hat, ejaculated " *Adios !* "

There was a certain benedictory flavor about this Spanish form of dismissal which, under the circumstances, was painfully irrelevant.

Our indignation at the bandit's delicate courtesy was in no sense lessened by the discovery, as we passed, that the dreaded accomplice had been improvised out of a hat, an old coat, a pair of trowsers and a forked sapling, which ingenious combination in the insincerity of the waning light bore a marked resemblance to a human figure.

The rhetoric of the party at this point was turbulent and impassioned, and ended in forcible denunciation of Belton Joe.

" P'raps ye'll reckon to drive four hosses and be able to give warnin' o' road-agints," said that worthy imperturbably. " Ef so, I'd like to go along with yer."

The effusive gentleman's reply, if violent, had at least the merit of sincerity. He forcibly suggested the advisability of the driver's journeying in a direction remote and unattainable, and expressed complete skepticism with reference to his future well-being.

Only the Judge displayed his customary equanimity. Quietly raising the cushion of the seat on which he sat, he took from a rent in its inner lining a plethoric wallet, and placed it complacently in the breast pocket of his coat.

Whereat the charming figure on the back
seat, which had during the recent confusion
displayed the feminine virtues of silence and a
snowy handkerchief, brightened up at once,
and congratulated him.

It was a very despondent and discordant
company that a half-hour later drove up at the
Cosmopolitan Hotel, Lampasas.

Notwithstanding its ambitious title, the
querulous proprietor was thrown into a temporary panic by the irruption of so many
guests at one time ; and the enforced doubling
up of the occupants of the primitive hostelry,
which was immediately ordered, argued unfavorably for our accommodation during the
night.   .

Neither were our depressed feelings alleviated
in any sense by a singular notice which was
posted on the walls, and stared conspicuously
at us as we were conducted to our several
rooms :

"Lowngers and Setters not Aloud on the
Stares."

The orthographic ambiguity of this abstract
statement haunted me for several days.

The additional discovery that our apartments were not furnished with lamps, and that all demands of the toilet were expected to be met by a tin wash-basin and a frouzy brush and comb in the bar-room, increased our discomfort.

Nevertheless, the spirit of gallantry was not quite crushed within us. We importuned the distressed landlord on the part of our fair companion, and finally succeeded in obtaining for her a hysterical hanging-lamp, that looked as if it would explode upon trifling provocation, and a delf wash-basin and water-pitcher, so pitifully handleless and broken-lipped as to entirely counteract the refreshing effect of the somewhat perfunctory ablutions they reluctantly afforded.

The Doctor dispatched to her assistance a small toilet-case which he luckily happened to have among his luggage, to which act of hospitality the Judge humanely added that of his pocket-flask, with the additional information that it was genuine Kentucky " Blue Grass."

It is probable that the sincerity of the Judge's belief in the potency of this article as a fortifier against pecuniary loss overbalanced his usual delicate discernment in feminine matters.

Nor was our respect for the fair one lessened when the last contribution was presently returned, to all appearances intact.

When we were finally summoned to supper by the ringing of a revolving bell, elevated upon a lofty derrick outside the hotel, and giving an impression of gratuitous public hospitality which the character of the viands alone could excuse, and had endeavored to satisfy the cravings of a long day's ride with the customary "yellow-ochre" biscuits and gravy-swimming bacon that were shoved at us through a long slit in the wainscot, on the other side of which these culinary triumphs were evidently achieved, the sentiment that our general discomfort had been sensibly aggravated was universal.

Not caring to join the group of natives who gathered dejectedly in the bar-room, about a red-hot box-stove, at which they vindictively spat, apparently in expressive criticism upon the recent meal, we soon retired.

A discretionary caution, fostered, no doubt, by a bird's-eye view of my quarters taken by daylight, led me to discard my pillow, as having been too privileged in its intimacy with a

previous occupant of the room, and to adopt
one extemporized of my boots rolled up in my
trowsers—an expedient with which my frontier
experience had long since made me familiar.

After a very brief interval of unconscious-
ness I awoke to a realizing sense of undigested
biscuits and a dyspeptic insomnia, aggravated
by my miserable surroundings.

It was a wild and gloomy night. I could hear
the wind outside buffeting the shaky structure,
charging the crazy shutters that opened on the
gallery, and communicating the violence of its
assault to the canvas partitions which insured
to the mutual confidences of guests of the Cosmopolitan Hotel the general privacy of a whispering gallery.

Lying broad awake and staring at the night
in utter hopelessness of sleep, I was abandoning
myself to despair, and possibly to anathema,
when I was diverted by the footsteps of two
belated revelers of Lampasas, evidently entering the next room, and about to go to bed.

At such times the most trivial details of our
neighbors are interesting, and I listened to the
hurried dragging of the bedclothes from the
bedstead, preliminary to the preferred camping-

out upon the floor—a peculiarity of Texan
lodgers which probably accounts for the general poverty of hotel bed-furnishings in the
State—with the satisfaction of novelty after my
previous monotonous vigil.

Then followed the kicking off of the lodgers'
boots, and immediately afterward, from the
stretching out of cramped limbs, the probable
settling of the occupants upon their lowly
couches.

The early rising of the native Texan is apparently inconsistent with an extensive night toilet.
After a short interval one of the men said, with
the air of renewing an interrupted conversation :

"Wal, ez thet the only place ye've been to,
to-day ?"

" No," replied the second, " I've been over to
Centrefitt."

" Ez *thet* so? Wot ev they doné with Jack
Bender ?"

Second Voice (ominously)—" Hung him !"

"Sho !"

" Fact ! "

" How'd he take it ?"

" Cool."

" Were you thar ? "

" You bet ! "

" Did he make any confession—squeal at all ? "

" Nary !—said he'd like to ketch thet wife of Jim White's, thet he fust met travelin' on the stage-coach, who got him soft on her, and then inter robbin' the mails."

First Voice—" Who'd he mean ? "

Second Voice—" Didn't ye never see her? "

" No ; wot's she like ? "

" Oh, she's a brewnette, putty as a picture, an' smarter nor a whip."

" Wot's she got ter do with it ? "

"Wal, she's a sorter pal o' Jim's; travels round, yer know, and keeps an eye to the passenger's valoobles, an' I reckon saves the necessity of ' divyin' ' up, bein' his wife, ye know."

First Voice—" Jack didn't hev nothin' to say about Jim, eh ? "

Second Voice—" Nothin'."

First Voice—" Didn't leave no dyin' words, nor any thin' ? "

Second Voice—" Wal, yes—he did too." (A laugh.) " Left a sorter crittercism on beer drinkin'. He was lookin' sorter glum and the

hangman—an accommodatin' **sort o'** cuss, outside o' his habit **o' tyin'** patent neck-ties—asked
him ef he couldn't **do** nothin' fur **him.   Jack**
sez :

"'**Yes,** I'd like a glass o' beer 'fore I go.'

" They brought it. Jack stood up, blowed the
foam off it, and drank **it.**   The hangman, bein'
a pryin' shrimp, sez :

"' **Jack,** I wanter **ax ye one** question.'

"' Sartin,' sez Jack.

"' Jes' tell me why ye blowed the foam **off**
thet yer beer, jest now.'

"'Wal,' says Jack, reflectin' like, 'it's *on-
healthy.*'

" They **strung him up** the next minit."

The humor **of** this *ante mortem* statement of
the unfortunate Jack seemed to affect both
narrator and auditor, **for** from that time **forward** nothing but subdued laughter filtered
through the partition.

Later, however, their deep drawn breathing
seemed **to** imply that it had an additional
soporific **quality.** Possibly its effect **upon my**
wakefulness may **have** been somewhat similar ;
for after **a** long interval, for which I was unable
to account by any positive train of **thought, I**

was aroused by what appeared to me to be the rustle of a woman's skirt in the narrow hallway. Eventually, however, I attributed it to the wind in the passage, and, turning upon my rude pillow, soon after fell asleep.

We waited the appearance of the fair one for some time at breakfast the next morning, and finally the Doctor was deputed to represent her admirers, and knock at her door.

To his astonishment the door was open, and the fair occupant of the bedroom *missing.*

So also was " Panhandle," the fleetest horse in the hotel proprietor's stables; and so also— as the enthusiastic Judge discovered later—was the plethoric wallet containing five thousand dollars in bank notes and checks, which he had so shrewdly rescued from the robbery of the day before.

I concluded that there must have been another interested listener to the mysterious dialogue of the previous night.

A WANDERING MELIBOEUS.

———o———

HE came to the ranch in a traveling "prairie schooner,"—a long, lank, bilious-looking individual, with hollow cheeks, deep, cavernous eyes, and a general flavor of despondency and gloom. He was still redolent of the town, and there was something so pretentious and aggressive about his stiff, narrow-brimmed Derby hat, his uncompromising city clothes, and his dreadfully soiled, but highly starched, Piccadilly collar, that he at once offended the frontier tastes of careless ranchmen.

The teamster beckoned to our foreman, and with an air of delivering questionable freight, became mysterious and confidential.

"I've brought ye out suthin'," said he, "which I reckon ye'll hev to brand ter form any opinion onter. 'Tain't no use guessin'. I've been figgerin' on him ever sençe I picked him up, an' I ain't decided yet whether he's a cur'osity or a drivelin' idjit, but I reckon it's both. Mebbe ye better put a bell onto him an' hobble him to onct, for he's thet gone here, (rubbing his forehead dubiously) thet he's likely to break loose an' give ye trouble. Sez he's goin' inter the sheep bizness. I wouldn't wonder ef he's been runnin' 'foot-loose' down at Tyler, an' hez got mooney over some gal ez he's been keepin' kempeny with. Enyway he's give me an earfull thet I don't reckon to git over by the time I git back. Don't let him git away with ye. *Adios!* G'lang!''

And with a portentous wink, diabolical in its implied necessity of caution, he whipped up his jaded mules—which were of the class inclined to lean back in the traces and think, as if debating whether a permanent halt were not advisable—and disappeared in the cloud of dust that veiled their refractory departure.

Meanwhile the new arrival had become suddenly invertebrate, and with both his long arms hitched over the gate of the ranch, had apparently hung himself up in a state of mental and physical collapse. He was gazing gloomily after the vanishing wagon. The suggestiveness of his attitude provoked the criticism of the camp.

"What's gone with that tramp?" inquired the "Oracle," who was thus recognized as a reluctant authority upon the sheep-question, and was disposed to be suspicious of all new-comers.

"Your complexion—I guess," replied our medical authority, who believed the Oracle to be suffering from torpidity of the liver, and was piqued at his refusal to submit to treatment.

"More likely he's struck some of those lightnin' pills you were mixin' the other night," retorted the Oracle.

As a matter of fact, the medical gentleman's acquaintance with the healing art was empirical rather than scientific. Having imported from the States a small medicine chest and an accompanying treatise, his diagnosis of a disorder was apt to be faulty and imperfect. Notably so in one particular instance. Since the Oracle had discovered that Menard was treating him for scurvy, when he was in reality suffering from weak eyes, he had been mildly skeptical in regard to the latter's knowledge. His communication of this trifling error to his companions had well-nigh relegated the practice of medicine at the ranch to the position of the lost arts.

But here was the longed for opportunity. Menard had already saddled his nose with the professional spectacles, and was deep in the perusal of attendant symptoms.

" Looks sorter gone in the epigastric region ; " he muttered to himself,—" yaller as saffron; eyes holler and fishy ; shouldn't wonder if his pulse might be feeble, and his tongue's coated, I'll bet a dollar against two bits. It's a sure case ! Blue mass—five pills at bed-time, and Turkey rhubarb—first thing in the morning. Here, Deacon, bring me out that medicine-chest ! "

But the individual addressed was busy prosecuting inquiries in regard to the new-comer on his own account.

"What's that you've got hung up on the gate ? " he inquired demurely of the foreman. "Somethin' new you've been inventin' for scarin' coyotes ? Don't believe it'll work ; hasn't *movement* enough. You can't expect to make any headway with a prairie-wolf, Ridge,

unless you show some signs of life. I supposed you had *savy* enough for that."

Ridge Johnson preserved his customary
gravity.

"Ye better go a little light on that feller,
Deak!" he responded—"he's a tenderfoot from
Tyler! come out with some gilt-edged notions
about the sheep business. I want a herder out
in "lone camp" up at the upper pecan-motte.
You just give me a couple of weeks, and I'll
get the flies off him."

It did not appear what the above expression
implied, nor how this presumably desirable result was to be attained, but we all had sufficient confidence in our foreman to possess our
souls in patience.

In the meantime, the medical gentleman had
approached the dejected figure by the gate,
and was apparently about to commence hostilities.

"You're feelin' a trifle caved-in," he said
pleasantly, but with a kind of professional deliberation; "your mouth tastes like a swill-
barrel, and your appetite's gone back on ye.
You don't sleep reg'lar, and things is on a general strike. You'd sell yourself out at a pretty

low figure, and take yer pay in parseley and
onions; so you jest naturally reckoned to come
out here and take a brace.   Young man, you've
got a large and level head!"

The man raised his lugubrious face to Menard's, mourned over him with his dreary, hopeless eyes, and said in a sepulchral voice,

" Yer right, pardner, I did."

" I *say*, you've struck it," replied Menard,
delightedly ; " you've run up against jest the
right party.   I'll have you a new man in twenty-
four hours."

The man looked up again with a shade of
interest in his face, and placing his hand on his
chest, asked anxiously :

" P'raps ye'll allow to hevin' hed a sorter
heaviness *here* thet smokin' didn't reach an'
feedin' wouldn't satisfy?   A kind o' feelin' as
ef ye'd lost half o' yerself, and yer inside was
goin' inter gin'ral bankrupsy?"

" Exactly!" said the gratified doctor—"that's
bile ! "

" Wha—a—at?" said the man, with a stare—
"you come off, pardner—it's *love !* "

" "Love?" echoed Menard, in amazement—
"Young man, you deceive yourself.   It's all

due to your liver. You see, it's been gettin'
too high-toned for the rest of your body.
You've been livin' pretty free, an' your diet has
jest filled it up with conceit, and it reckons now
to lay by, and see how you'll make it go without it. What you want to do, my friend, is to
submit yourself to me. I've got a patent pill
in there, that'll make you think——"

"Ye jest oughter get to see her," broke in
the man vacantly, entirely ignoring Menard's
graphic statement of the alarming condition of
his domestic economy—" ye jest oughter get to
see her! the sweetest, prettiest, lovin'est cree-
tur ye ever set yer two eyes on. And Lord
love ye! no end o' style. Why, when me an'
her useter walk out on Main Street of a Sun-
day arternoon, the way fellers useter turn
roun' and stare, was a reg'lar show. And high-
toned too, you bet! She's the niece of an ex-
Guv'ner of the State. I useter say to her—
'Mirandy,' sez I, 'thet a top-notch and A. 1.
girl like you should get gone on such a chap ez
me is what gits me!' An' she useter say to
me—'William Henry'—she allus went fur my
hull name—thet's Mirandy—'it was yer height
an' yer gin'ral shape that fust got away with
me!'"

The Doctor turned away in disgust.

"Aren't ye gettin' about tired of importin' these desperate characters and professional dead-beats from the southern country?" he inquired of the foreman. "The last man you had was wanted down at San Antone for horse-stealin', and I wouldn't insure this new invoice against any bad spell of weather. Just look at him ventilatin' himself out thar on thet fence, and invitin' the attention of every enterprisin' buzzard. The first good 'Norther' we have will freeze him up so stiff we won't have any use for him except to stop the gap in a brush-pen."

But the conviction was so general that the Doctor was right for once, that discussion was out of the question, and Menard walked deject-edly away to his tent. Being a punctiliously honorable man, it did not occur to him to en-tertain the camp with the gentleman's own theory of his despondent condition. He pre-ferred to regard it in the light of a privileged communication—probably induced by dyspep-sia—and as such to be held inviolate by an as-pirant in his learned profession.

Later he had an opportunity of noting the

alarming waste of **tissue** presumably **due to this** morbid activity **of the** affections.

This was at dinner, when in common with **us** all, he lamented the frequency with which our guest passed his plate, and the surprising facility with which the four staples of ranch-life— bread, bacon, beans, and stewed-apples—disappeared to fill an insatiable vacuum. Indeed, **the capacity of** William Henry Smack, **as it recurs to** me at this remote epoch, is a subject for unhallowed meditation. That appears to have been **the** infelicitous title with which **his** unfortunate sponsors decided **to honor the** planet. From association with **his** collapsed personality, **it gave you a** disagreeable impression that **they had started** him fairly and **then run him** into something—his *appetite*, **the** Oracle suggested. It was even thoughtfully recom. mended to me by this sardonic joker,—who sat next to William Henry at table, and had been amusing himself by depositing various indigestible articles in the neighborhood **of his** plate, and watching **him** successively **reject** them—to start **him on the dried apple sack.** **and** then kindly suggest **hot** water **as** an assist· **ant** to digestion. **But** although **during his**

short sojourn with us, Smack frequently repaired to me for advice, I do not recall that he
ever confessed to any gastric disturbance.

It was shortly after this phenomenal meal
that I first attracted his attention and invited
his confidence. I was at that time suffering an
unhallowed martyrdom—a martyrdom that recurs upon the frontier with the regularity of a
repeating cycle—attended by burned fingers,
outraged patience and occasional profanity. I
was taking my turn as *cook*. Over an abyss of
steaming dish-water, and a discouraging waste
of disorganized plates, knives, and forks, I extended to him the hand of sympathy, and an
unusually clean portion of flour-sack, and invited
his coöperation in the agreeable task of wiping
dishes.

He had been prowling aimlessly about the
ranch with his hands in his pockets, but I regret to say, with a seeking-whom-he-may-de-
vour expression on his melancholy visage that
was apparently visited by my associates with
ill-favor and exclusion. I am a sympathetic man.
It occurred to me that there was nothing
particularly prepossessing about such an introduction to sheep-farming as Mr. Smack had

received. It did *not* occur to me that there was any thing sufficiently prepossessing about Mr. Smack to warrant any other state of facts. But I resolved to waive this on the score of humanity. I little knew what was in store for me.

"I reckon, now, you fellers left a heap o' society back there in the States," he began, as he unguardedly accepted a red-hot dish in his naked hand.

I nodded a tacit assent.

"Any gals?" he inquired, shifting the dish rapidly from one hand to the other, and alternately snapping his fingers.

In the midst of my anxiety for the future of our big platter, a vision of dear Leonora, as she appeared when bidding me adieu at the steamer's wharf, flashed across my excited consciousness and faded utterly, as the dish caromed on the table suddenly, glanced to the floor, and dispersed in far reaching and magnificent ruin.

"It's the only one on the ranch," I remarked ungraciously, as he gazed hopelessly upon the glittering fragments.

"Haven't ye got any *strayteener?*" he inquired absently.

This was adding insult to injury—suggesting the possession of such an article to persons only two years behind the Indians. I retaliated sharply.

"Why Lord love ye!" he said, seeing my evident disgust,—"ye can get it at any street corner down in Tyler!"

"My Christian friend," said I, in a blaze of wrath,—"when you get out in 'lone camp' on the bald prairie, with no company but your dog, a six-by-nine tent, and a 'wet Norther' howling down from Kansas at the rate of sixty miles an hour, it will perhaps occur to you that you can't go to the corner grocery every time you're out of matches and soap."

For some minutes the dish-washing progressed in silence.

At length, raising his head slowly, after long and apparently earnest cogitation,

"Got any picters?" he inquired.

"Pictures of what?" I asked with some acerbity of tone—suggestive of the perishability of crockery.

"Of them Eastern gals o' yours," he replied solemnly.

Again, a vision of the absent Leonora, with

her faultless features and fashionable attire, rescued from oblivion by Eastern photography, and hidden from vulgar scrutiny in the remotest recesses of my trunk, came vividly before me.

I modestly acknowledged the possession of a few.

"Light or dark-complected?" said my cross-examiner.

"All colors," I retorted with shameless mendacity.

"I want to know!" he ejaculated in amazement, and with an apparent willingness to believe that there might be types of beauty of a character unknown to him;—"I want to know!   .

"Wal! Mirandy's light, an' I jes' nat'rally get my notions on thet subject from her. She *is* a honey-cooler, pardner, and don't you forget it. When she togs out and takes to promenadin' you better reckon she paints the hull town red. Some day, when you've got a plenty of time, I'd like to put her picter up agin the best gals you can show, and see Mirandy walk away with the outfit. I'll read ye all her letters too, and show ye what a writer she is. Thar! Cast yer eye over thet yer! How does thet strike ye?"

And he threw down upon the table a tin-type of the siren who had inspired the previous harangue.

I wish the reader might have seen Mirandy. Being ignorant myself of the precise amount of feminine charm necessary to impart a sanguinary coloring to the average Texan town, I can not, of course, express the opinion that the young lady met the requirements. But if the zeal of the artist, in atoning for the neutral tints of his art by embellishing her natural graces with highly rouged cheeks, a green feather, a pink bow, and the crowning triumph of old-gold gaiters, were insufficient to the task, ah, me! I fear this feeble pen had best not attempt to do justice to this social paragon. Perhaps I may better convey the extravagance of my own appreciation, by expressing a faint hope that the photographer escaped with his instrument intact. I recollect that the Oracle, before whom her charms were paraded on a later occasion, remarked to me in confidence that he "should like to have that face to stamp tubs of butter." But the Oracle was given to sar-

casm, and the idea of butter upon a frontier
ranch was so wildly imaginative, that it is possible some latent compliment to the worshiped
Mirandy may have been intended.

It was early spring in the little valley. There
were signs of resurrection in the levels and on
the divides. The sentinel mesquites timidly
displayed their emerald epaulettes, and gave
glimpses of their summer uniform, as if still
reluctant to appear on dress-parade ; but the
bold live oaks threw off their faded fatigue-
jackets, and challenged Nature in full panoply.
Already a delicate housing of green enamel
decked the gaunt flanks of the distant hills.
The sunny slopes were glad with waving color
and springing grasses. The ravages of winter
were repaired by the coy visits of blue lupins,
poppy worts of red and orange, and the rarer
glories of the golden helianthus. Over gay
corollas of every tint and shade, the red-
bird flashed, the scissor-tail piloted his trailing plumes, and the southern nightingale—
that mad ventriloquist in white and sable—
mocked and wantoned. In the mellow light of
lengthening days, and on the mighty trunks of
majestic pecans, the flaming yellow-hammer

was busy with his undertaking, and the burial
of the dead season was announced in the dim
aisles by the repeated knocking of his dismal
mallet.

And then the stern spirit of the dying monarch entered his protest, and forbade the
ceremony. The ghost of his troubled greatness
stirred in the North, struggling back in an
ominous cloud, that suddenly spread and hid
the frightened heavens with gray. The icy
gasps of the indignant Shade came quick and
fast, blighting the early promise of spring, and
sending the thermometer down thirty degrees
in as many minutes. And with them came a
host of avenging spirits—shrieking winds,
hurrying rain, and blinding sleet, that locked
the borders of the shallow creeks; clapped an
icy mail on the northward bark of trees and
bushes; caught and crystallized drooping flower
and budding spray, and drove the bleating stock
to the shelter of corrals, and their shivering
shepherds to the protection of yellow "slickers."

The branches bowed and broke with their
weight of fringing icicles; bereavement sad-
dened the wretched birds; destruction was in

the air; and the stark landscape lay white and ghastly in the pallor of its desolation.

But during the rigor of this untimely Norther, fate was yet kind to William Henry. Either a growing compassion for Mirandy's woful knight, or more probably, a manifest reluctance to intrust a flock of giddy yearlings to the tutelage of so painful a tenderfoot, restrained our foreman from initiating him unkindly into the mysteries of his new vocation. Throughout the gloomy, dismal days the coziest corner of the kitchen-stove was occupied by this rare and delicate exotic of the interior.

Of course this tendency to take root, and blossom in perpetual reminiscence of Mirandy, was met with unkindly criticism, and even on some occasions with impolite objurgation. It was generally believed that he had overheard the Doctor's prediction of his possible utility at this disagreeable season, and that he resolved to forestall him by inhabiting localities of perpetual thaw.

I am afraid that even my sympathetic nature grew weary of Mr. Smack. After I had learned that he was a tanner by trade, and had gotten over my surprise that devotion to his profession

had left him so unaccountably with this " perennial virginity of the affections," a continuous
rehearsal of the various phenomena which attended the appearance of the absent goddess
upon the public streets of Tyler lost somehow
its power of diversion. Perhaps my feelings
may have been influenced by observing that
any assistance in my labors from William
Henry was invariably attended by culinary disaster, or mortality in the cupboard, and if I refrained from any open allusion to his customary seat, I fear that a warmer locality than the
kitchen-stove was the direct wish of my inner
consciousness.

But it was gratifying to witness the devices
to which my associates would resort to decoy
him from his corner and to destroy his statuesque
repose. The Doctor had an elaborate inven-
tion for catching quail which consisted of an
old salt-sack and a tallow candle, and, calling
him one day into his tent, he promised that if
on the first mild night, William Henry would
engage to hold this lighted candle in front of
the aperture of the sack, surprising results might
be attained that would redound to an im-
provement of the larder—the monotony of

which Mr. Smack had already alluded to, but with no appreciative diminution of consumptive capacity. Then the Oracle, who was an authority on sheep matters, explained very minutely the uses of the crook, telling this guileless innocent that in catching a sheep the curving portion must be applied to the lower jaw, and by a dexterous movement of the operator the animal laid upon his back; but that when bare-handed, the ears were the coveted objects of attack.

And I have an amusing recollection of how the Deacon, on one occasion, exhibited, for his absorbed inspection, an extensive assortment of variety actresses, informing him that they were the portraits of young ladies who, in better days, had succumbed to his delusive arts, and being base enough to assert afterwards that the munificent graces of a certain song and dance *artiste* had for the time being staggered his faith in the ideal charms of Mirandy.

I think, however, I am myself responsible for first opening his eyes to the austerities of life upon the frontier. It had been decided that I should have his companionship during those hours when a sensitive man is presumably most fastidious in matters of companionship. The shelter, hitherto sacred to Morpheus and myself, was a small tent, pitched upon a lonely hillside, in the neighborhood of a primitive brush-pen, where the flock, that in future was to engage the attention of William Henry, was also accustomed to pass the night.

On the evening of the Norther's advent, I lighted a little dark lantern that I sometimes carried, and prepared to resort to my quarters. Being in no very amiable mood at the prospect before me, I resolved to try the nerves of my prospective bed-fellow, and drawing the slide of my lantern and slipping it under my long " slicker," I called him from the seclusion of the stove, and strode out into the night.

It was pitch dark—not even the caverns of Erebus can hope to rival the blackness of a Norther's night. It is immoral in its quality, and in its effect upon the rhetoric of the wayfarer. And through the gloom, the fiery darts of the sleet splinter and sting, and the mad blasts howl with the fury of fiends.

Such being the case, I must confess it was with malice aforethought that, as we fared on together, I expressed a cheerful hope that he would not fall into the well, which with that sublime confidence in animate and inanimate nature peculiar to Texas, is generally left guilt-less of environment. There was no reply to this, but I am quite sure I detected a slight gasp at the prospect of such a possibility.

Shortly after, Mirandy's champion going astray in the gloom, and missing the echo of my accompanying step, became so unpleasantly vocal, that I was forced to display my light to silence him. Joining forces again, we pro-ceeded in company until we reached the tent.

Being desirous of exhibiting a unique and beautiful effect, I unmasked my lantern in the direction of the pen, and invited his attention. The far reaching rays of light were reflected from the eye-balls of the sheep, glancing in every direction over a gleaming pavement of orbs, and flashing upon us in globes of fire. And here I know not what panic seized Mr. Smack, but with a wild cry of alarm, he dashed the lantern from my hand and ran off into the night, shouting and screaming at the top of his lungs. The immediate result of which was a startling irruption of the occupants of the ranch, armed with " six-shooters," and bearing lantern and torch, in anticipation of a violent attack on the part of coyotes.

For three days the pitiless javelins of the sleet beleaguered hill and hollow with storm and assault. For three days the incautious heads of early risers, striking against the sloping roof-trees of their tents, were startled by the crepitant recoil, and the hurrying crash of the hurtling avalanche which followed. For three days the tortured Winter writhed and raved in its delirium, moaning through the hollow valleys, and tossing in impotent fury its cramped and stiffened limbs. Then came the stillness of death. The sun looked through the rifted clouds and saw the wasted form of the fallen monarch lying in its last sleep. Every bush and shrub and tree was bowed to the earth as with the weight of a mighty grief. And then from out the heart of the benign Mother, a deep emotional whisper reassured her children; their cares dissolved and slipped away, and spring was welcomed anew, but between smiles and tears.

Mr. Smack was no sharer in the general enthusiasm at the ranch. A lengthy consultation with our foreman, relative to the locality of his future labors, seemed to have accented his habitual melancholy. It is possible that the prospect of a month's sheep herding, in the solitude of his own society, may have unconsciously aggravated the remoteness of Mirandy. After a patient and long-suffering perusal of the correspondence of that beloved maiden, I had become skeptical in regard to her high social position. There was an originality in orthography, and an absence of punctuation about her efforts, which I had not hitherto detected in the nieces of senators and governors. Possibly the epistolary style of the first families may have deteriorated.

In a moment of irritation over her reiterated fascinations and accomplishments, I had maliciously inquired how he came to deprive himself of such excellence. His reply, I fear, embodies the experience of many a gilded youth, and has the glamour of a too prevalent popular fallacy. It seems that Mirandy's refined taste in jewelry and surprising saccharine longings absorbed his weekly salary, and he had resorted to a sheep-camp for the accumulation of a fortune wherewith to embark upon the matrimonial sea. I could not repress a sigh as I realized how enormous would be his harvest of blighted hopes.

O city clerks! plying a ready and facile quill, beware how you entertain the chimera of sudden wealth in the far West! Unless your pockets are heavy with the shekels of past gains, and you have the requisite cash and experience with which to invest—just as you may at home, if haply ye be so circumstanced —seek not to penetrate this arcana of hardship and disappointment. Remember that over a dreary waste of fried bacon and corn-dodger, and amid grievous solitude, will this experience come to you, and that the prospect of becoming a capitalist, upon twenty dollars a month, is remote even upon the frontier.

I did not witness the departure of William Henry for the upper pecan-motte, but I am informed that he pulled himself together, and with the air of an heroic general rallying panic-stricken troops, set out in pursuit of his flying cohorts. I believe the Deacon said something about a rapid degeneration of the flock to nothing but hides and hoofs, if he continued to herd upon the full gallop, but the Deacon had a sick headache that day, and at such times his judgment was jaundiced.

The following morning, while making my customary early pilgrimage from my sleeping apartment to the kitchen, I noticed a peculiar demonstration upon the western horizon. It was unlike any thing in movement I had yet witnessed. There were certain suggestions of the windmill about it, but I knew that we had perfected no such method of irrigation. There seemed to come to my ears from the depths of this mystery a feeble halloo. With much straining of my eyes, I at last perceived that it was William Henry, swinging his boots by their straps like a pair of erratic Indian clubs. He had evolved this unique signal as a species of decoy for me. I repaired to the spot.

But if his signal was unique, what shall I say of his appearance? Certainly no damsel but fair Bettina, or that "maiden all forlorn" who espoused the modern tramp of the nursery legend, would have ever dreamed of accepting his escort.

He was in his stocking feet; his smart city suit was in ribbons; I hesitate to record how many cruel stabs that immaculate Derby had sustained from the thorns of the mesquite. It was at once ludicrous and pitiful to hear him

describe, how, while following his flock in full
cry, he had stumbled in a marmot burrow, and
sat down upon an aggressive cactus.

"It's no use!" he exclaimed, as I regarded
him in breathless awe; "I'm goin' to quit!
They've been junein' me sence yesterday
mornin', all over the bald prairie, an' last night I
didn't get a wink o' sleep listenin' to the
coyotes. Some wild cows got into my tent
yesterday, eat up my grub, and made a stampin'
ground of the hull bizness. I've been as hungry as a prairie dog, and as lonely as a turtle
on a log, all night."

"Couldn't you occupy your mind in thinking
of that girl of yours?" I inquired with malicious irony.

"That's jest it!" he shrieked, with a despondent wave of the boots—"I've been figgerin' how on earth I'm ever goin' to get a letter from her 'way out here, an' mebbe, all the
while, some one o' them julery sharps is cut-
tin' me out. I reckon I'll go hum. Ye needn't
pay me nothin'. It's no use! *I tell ye, I'm
goin' to quit!*"

And out of respect for his accident, he descended slowly upon his knees, and attempted

the perilous feat of drawing on his boots while in that position.

I expostulated with him for a long time, urging that our foreman had gone to town, and that it was impossible to pen the sheep and let them starve during the day. At last upon my promising that, if he would continue to herd until Johnson's return, I would come up to camp and spend the night with him, he reluctantly consented. I returned to the ranch.

It was a cool, pleasant evening, when I started with "Top"—a favorite sheep-dog—to fulfill my promise. The Milky Way hung high in heaven, and the air was full of the shrill chirp of crickets, and the cry of cicadæ. The fragrant odors of the season were abroad again, and came sweetly from the damp wings of night. But I needed all the consolations of the time. A series of misfortunes, beginning with burnt beans, and culminating in the discovery of Dr. Menard, lost in the perusal of his medical treatise, and seated absently upon a rising batch of bread which I had laboriously prepared after a new receipt, had wrought their accepted havoc upon my outraged feelings.

As I drew near the lone camp, the moon

lifted a pale crescent above the tops of the great pecans, illuminating with silver the gaunt outlines of a large cow-pen that stretched beneath them. Startled by my approach, the sheep stampeded into the shadows of their roomy barrier, and a frightened bevy of quail whirred across my path. The white tent gleamed through the dim spaces of the trees, like an odd transparency.

"I made up my mind ye was goin' back on me!" remarked William Henry grimly, as I entered.

"How are you?" I inquired vaguely, throwing myself into a corner and pillowing my head upon a sack of coffee.

"Most dead," he replied cheerfully.

"How did your sheep herd to-day?"

"About as near like a lot of crazy mules as they could—convenient."

"Any trouble from wolves?"

"I reckon they'll be on hand, as soon as I make for bed."

"Hungry?" said I, exhibiting a large basket.

"Jest starvin'," he replied.

"Did it ever occur to you, William?" said I, as he attacked the provender with both hands,

—"that in business as in love there is no success with a faint heart?"

"How far is it from here to Paint Rock?" he inquired, evading the issue.

"Thirty-five miles."

"Which way?"

"Due west," I said, giving him the line.

"And San Saba?"

"About sixty—off here!

"I hope, however," said I, "that you are not contemplating the journey on foot, for the chances are, that with your inexperience of the country, you would lose your way and perish miserably."

He did not reply, but lay knocking his heels together and caressing "Top." Subsequently, when he artfully intruded a thread-bare subject by insinuating a love-letter that I already knew by heart, I wrapped myself in my blanket and went calmly to sleep.

We awoke betimes the next morning, and after a primitive repast, released the imprisoned sheep. As I stood looking at them grazing away in beautiful company-front, and with the far-reaching wings of their slowly moving column stretching over the flowering prairie in

admirable order, I was impressed that they
were the best herding yearlings I had ever
seen.

" Do you mind lending me this dog?" said
William Henry, "they *run so*, you know."

More out of compassion for his loneliness
than any other reason, I consented. We parted
company on the next divide. I never saw him
again.

For when our foreman returned at noon and
visited the lone camp, he found the sheep bleating in the pen ; the collapsed tent flying in the
wind ; the sticky equipment of that early breakfast broiling in the sun. But all traces of food,
or dog, or William Henry, were irrevocably
gone.

I think of him tenderly yet. Time has con-
soled me for the loss of my dog, and a dearth
of correspondence on the part of Leonora has
made me more charitable in my estimate of his
trials. There are times, when, over a tranquil
pipe, and under the witchery of moonlight, the
memory of his soulful devotion affects me with
the pathos of knight-errantry. And if, perchance,
within some wooded copse or thorny chaparral,
the bleaching bones of this misguided and wan-

dering Melibœus of the South nave found no
mourners save the hooting owl and gaunt coyote, I have, at least, the consciousness of having
warned him, and his untimely fate is but the
sad sequel of his own temerity.

But I do not like to think of him thus. I
prefer rather to reflect upon the ubiquity of
wandering teamsters and their attendant mules.
And oft, before my fancy, rises a picture of a
respectable tanner, with children playing around
his knees, and a father's pride illuminating his
hollow eyes, and by his side a grave and quiet
matron, in whose subdued appearance you
might seek in vain, for traces of the saccharine
tastes and jewel-loving extravagance of the beloved Mirandy.

A FRONTIER BOHEMIAN.

THE sun was setting on the Maverick valley. As I walked to the door of the ranch, a few Parthian arrows from his declining bow splintered themselves among the dusky tops of the live oaks. There was a faint pink glow all around the horizon that on its western threshold lingered in feathery flecks of crimson and gold. The brief twilight of Texan latitudes was already hastening through the thin files of mesquite that stood like straggling pickets before the windows of the little cabin. A silence was falling over the hushed landscape — " vast, measureless, complete."

Certainly I had some excuse for the sudden loneliness that fell upon me. It was the first time in my border life that I had been left upon the trackless prairie, solitary and alone. The annual shearing was just over. But an hour before our entire " outfit" had **departed for a** general merry-making **at a** distant frontier town. As I had volunteered in accepting the **position of cook** during **the past** three weeks, and for **that** period had labored to fill a recurrent and appalling vacuum in eighteen able-bodied men, **my** efforts had naturally **been** somewhat debilitating. Amid **that exuberance of society in** which solitude seems **a** myth, **I had** declined conviviality **and** elected repose. **I was** left behind as custodian of the ranch.

But as I stepped **from the door for the pur-**pose of penning the **buck-herd, I** was beginning to regret my **choice. I** realized that I—a "tenderfoot "—**with** only **a** three months' residence in the state—was alone upon an area of **fifty thousand acres** without let or limit; that my nearest neighbor was five miles away, **over** a chartless, emerald sea, to **be** traversed only by aid of that shifting guide, the sun; **that my** only companions in this primitive wilderness were thirty-five Merino bucks of contemplative and exclusive tendencies ; a shepherd-dog which was immaturely effusive **and** slobberingly demonstrative upon **being** addressed **as** " Miss **Flo "; and an** ebony cat that inflicted a mangy and somewhat dissipated exterior under the sobriquet of "Miss Emma." A dearth of the consolations of female society apparently inspires the native Texan to a courteous acknowledgment of the sex of domestic pets.

When, therefore, I had driven the horned contingent of my associates into their rude brush-pen, and had fastened the hurdle-gate, I stood leaning against it and seriously regarding them. It did not add to the cheerfulness of my surroundings to notice that they bore an unmistakable resemblance to a company of hook-nosed Jews; that their knees were sprung with the rheumatism of age; that their eyes were rheumy and inflamed; and that they appeared to be unusually afflicted that evening with snuffles and chronic catarrh. Besides, they were so fresh from the shears, that the air of venerable wisdom which their faces arrogated, seemed to be caricatured by the rest of their bodies. They were so repulsive in appearance, that I at once dubbed the most disreputable specimen, "Fagin,"—a baptismal inspiration that eventually achieved popularity. Then, with that hypocrisy which characterizes man when lonely, I began to patronize my

much abused dog and even the feline antique;
for both had accompanied me in my pastoral
duties. After which I walked back to the
ranch. Here I encountered another dubious
object that in my then dejected condition struck
me as almost ominous. This was a pet lizard
which, for the past month, had inhabited the
neighboring kitchen—a long, low structure with
a canvas roof—and which was now perched
upon the door-step. But "Tommy" was on
the present occasion very much out of luck.
He was not under the most favorable circumstances a prepossessing object. He was brick-
red, covered with polka-dots of black, and had
a diabolical leer about the eye. "Tommy,"
however, had now unaccountably lost his tail,
and was obviously so humiliated and dispirited,
that he unconsciously infected and aggravated
my own melancholy.

I opened the door of the kitchen into which
he immediately dived and hid his diminished
lizardship from view. Entering the little cabin,
and acting from a feeling of generous hospitality
that must have struck both as phenomenal, I
invited the companionship of "Miss Flo" and
"Miss Emma." Then I lighted the lamp, and

drawing the solitary chair of the apartment to a convenient distance, picked up a volume of Macaulay's Essays (for we were fortunately blessed with an abundance of literature), and disposed myself to read. I remember thinking, as I settled myself into a comfortable position, that I would make amends for my enforced isolation by profound literary culture, and rather pluming myself upon how much benefit I should derive from this prairie course of study. But I certainly made little progress that evening. I found myself singularly unable to concentrate my attention. I was oppressed by an indefinable feeling of dread that at last culminated in a nervous sensation of being observed. I threw aside my book in disgust and endeavored to account for it.

It was now pitch dark outside. I was sitting at a little desk that, from the poverty of our household furniture, was obliged to perform manifold duties. To-night it was somewhat overburdened with frontier bric-a-brac, conspicuous among which was a large Colt's revolver and cartridge-belt. I perceived that, as I sat, I was directly in line with the two windows of the ranch—one on the south, the other on the

north side of the house. Partly from a feeling
of caution which one acquires on the frontier,
and partly from this nervousness I could not
explain, I shifted my chair around against the
wall until I faced the southern window. In
effecting this change of position, I succeeded
in treading on Miss Emma, and discommoding
Miss Flo, who, after looking at me in a grieved
fashion, accommodated herself in another
quarter with the usual canine philosophy and
circumlocution.

As I tilted my chair against the door and as-
sumed an aggressive attitude towards the opposite window, I noticed a few drops of water
upon the panes, and was then for the first time
aware that it was raining. A moment after a
vivid flash of lightning illuminated the darkness
without, opening up phosphorescent vistas in
the mesquites with startling suddenness. Brief
as was the interval for observation, it was sufficient to confirm my suspicions. Amid the loud
reverberations of the thunder-clap that followed,
I was confident that I had seen a man lurking
in the scanty shrubbery outside.

I cannot describe how much I was discon-
certed by this discovery. I was alone in a wild and

lawless country, where a man might be attacked
and murdered without a chance of succor. I
was in a lighted room whose unshuttered windows stared into the black night so glaringly,
that practically I was as defenseless to an
enemy hid in the darkness without, as if shut in
a glass case. As this thought leaped to my
brain, I suddenly extinguished the light and
groped for the revolver and cartridge-belt, re-
solving to make as determined a stand as possible. Securing both, I buckled on the belt and
backed against the door, in order to resist any
forcible entrance. In this defiant attitude I
waited, the storm continuing to rage without.

A Texan thunderstorm is at all times awe-
inspiring. I do not think I ever lived a more
thrilling existence than during the brief interval I crouched in the darkness of that little
cabin, which was incessantly lighted by the blue
flashes that seemed to leap from window to
window, and which shook tremulously under
the crash of the shattering reports that followed one another in quick succession. My
excitement reached its height, when, during
one of these sudden illuminations, I perceived

pressed against the pane and peering into the room, a wild, red face, with long, gray beard and disheveled hair streaming in the wind. The apparition, seen by the lurid light, was so malevolent, that I think I was only prevented from firing at it by the brief interval of the flash. When the lightning gleamed again, the face was gone, and I was certain now I could hear some one groping his way along the side of the house, evidently supporting himself in that way against the charging gusts of wind and sharp fusillade of the driving rain. At the same time Miss Flo became uneasy, and, at last, barked loudly.

"Hulloa, here!" shouted a gruff voice.

I hastily relighted the lamp, and opened the door in some trepidation.

There entered a tall figure, so gratuitously limp and bedraggled with rain as to be almost grotesque; so worn with travel, and with such an utter weariness of life in the eyes, as to be really pathetic. The clothes that he wore were torn and abraded, exposing a sub-stratum of red flannel at the knees, which gave him a ludicrous suggestion of having worn himself down to the quick from the excess of his devotions. His shrunken pantaloons encroached upon the calves of his legs, and, as he was without stockings, this lack of intimacy with his hob-nailed shoes exposed a pair of very gaunt and reluctant ankles. His beard and hair were long, straggling, and unkempt, and were surmounted by an extravagant slouch hat of the frontier pattern. Running over the scant details of my former apparition, I mentally classified him at once as a " border tramp." But I was lonely that evening and disposed to be polite. I therefore offered him the only chair in the room, stretched myself upon the low bed, and calmly awaited developments.

" Good evening," he said, in a rather husky but pleasant voice, as he lapsed into the chair. Then he took off his broad hat with a swirl of spattering rain-drops, wiped his forehead with a red bandana handkerchief, ruminated a few minutes, replaced his hat, and finally producing a pipe and a plug of tobacco, began slowly cutting up and crumbling the latter—the usual frontier preliminaries to a smoke.

I watched his movements with absorbing interest. He reminded me so forcibly of pictures of the lamented John Brown, that I was more than ever inclined to accept the "singular conflicting conditions of that martyr's soul and body," as exemplified in the popular song.

When he had finally lighted his pipe and emitted several curling rings of smoke, this singular figure vouchsafed the information that he had come across country in the hope of assisting us in shearing. I informed him that we had just finished that day for the season. He seemed to experience some regret at this, and for a time smoked on in silence. At length, his eyes happening to fall upon my relinquished volume, he took it up, glanced over it hastily, and laid it down again.

"You have been reading Macaulay?" he said. I assented in some surprise.

"Ah!" said my strange guest,— "A wonderful man! a wonderful man, that same Macaulay! What a genius, what learning, what a noble style he had, to be sure!"

Then throwing his head back and narrowing his wild eyes, he suddenly broke out:

"'An acre in Middlesex is worth a principality in Utopia; the smallest actual good is better than the most magnificent promises of impossibilities; the wise man of the Stoics would, no doubt, be a grander object than a steam engine. But there are steam engines. And the wise man of the Stoics is yet to be born. A philosophy which should enable a man to feel perfectly happy when in agonies of pain may be better than a philosophy that can assuage pain. But we know that there are remedies that will assuage pain; and we know that the ancient sages liked the toothache as little as their neighbors.'"

I sat up at this effort of memory in some amazement. For the past three months, having associated with individuals whose vocabularies hardly ventured beyond the possibilities of "right smart" and "away over yonder," I was somewhat startled, I admit.

"Are you a native of the state, sir?" I asked with great respect.

"No," replied he, turning full upon me for an instant those singular eyes of his,—"I am, like yourself, a Northerner."

"Let me offer you a better pipe," I said, pointing out to him the case containing my best meerschaum. "You will find some excellent 'Cavendish' in that jar."

He gave me a quick glance, as if appreciative of my hospitality, but declined, saying that long habit had given him a preference for the natural leaf.

"What is your college?" he suddenly asked, as I was filling a pipe preparatory to joining him.

"Yale," I answered with the pardonable pride of all sons of that *alma mater*,—and yours?"

"I seldom mistake a collegian," remarked my incongruous visitor— "'*Infandum, Regina, jubes renovare dolorem.*' I hail from Dartmouth."

I had made the inquiry more from politeness than any other motive, and yet, at the moment of my speaking, it flashed across me that he must be college-bred. Now that I was assured of it, I felt a sincere regret in seeing one who had enjoyed such advantages, at such wretched odds with fortune. He must have divined what passed through my mind, for he glanced hurriedly—and half sadly, as it seemed to me— over his forlorn garments, and then raising his eyes to mine, and with a gleam of humor lurking beneath his shaggy brows, said,

"And, pray, sir, how came a gentleman of your education and intelligence down in this God-forsaken country?"

I smiled, and attributed my advent to the adventurous spirit of the nineteenth century, for want of a better reason. He took my answer in the spirit in which it was given, and appeared in a sense to be relieved by it, as if it established a bond of union between us, it struck me. But he resisted all inquiries of mine into his antecedents or past history, meeting my hints and questions with adroit evasion and skillful changes of the subject.

And so, in the quiet night—for the rain had now ceased, and the moon, riding high, silvered the wan landscape, and fringed the dripping foliage with flashing gems—we drifted back to the topic with which we began and talked of literary themes. It has been my privilege to converse with not a few cultured and learned men, and to enjoy the society of some of the most brilliant of modern conversationalists, but as I sat and listened that evening to the words that fell from the lips of this frontier bohemian, it seemed to me that my acquaintance with the nature of true eloquence had just begun. It

was "like reading **Homer** by flashes of lightning." What **a** wealth **of** bold imagery, **of**
keen appreciation, **of** suggestive analogy, **of**
marvelous insight was **there**! And what a
treasure house **of** memory! And when he
finally lapsed into monologue, and indulging
in **a** rhapsody **upon** the wonders of Milton,
quoted from "**Paradise Lost**" **by** paragraph
and page, I thought of Macaulay's boast that
if the great poet's immortal **epic** should by any
chance **be** lost **to** men, he might **hope to re-**
produce it; and my admiration for the attain-
ments of **the man** swept over me in one vast
wave of **wonder**. And then, as **I** lay there,
listening **to his** deep voice which had grown
singularly rich and sonorous, as if **in sympathy**
with **the** dignity of **those** grand **periods**, pondering what strange chance or force of circumstance **had** compelled this incongruous being
to such surroundings, his form suddenly dilated,
his lips parted as if in terror, his eyes became
fixed on vacancy and staring, and with a sudden
spring to **his feet,** he stood erect and menacing.

  "Avaunt!" he cried, gazing **with a wild** and
frenzied stare into **the empty air,**—"Avaunt!
and quit my sight! Begone, I say! **Think'st**

thou to dog my footsteps always? To hound
me to the day of my death? Back! Back!
G-r-r-rhr! Take your grip from off my neck!
Avaunt!"

He dashed his hands to his throat, clutching
it wildly, and striding to the door, flung it wide
open, glaring long and fiercely out into the
quiet night with a frenzied and hunted expression. Then he came slowly back to the table,
tottering feebly and muttering incoherently,
threw himself into his chair, and covering his
haggard face with both his trembling hands,
shuddered and gasped alternately. Great beads
of agony stood upon his brow.

I was so startled by this sudden outburst
that I could only stare and sit speechless. When
he first rose I was under the impression that it
was to give greater force to some terrific denunciation. Not until he tore open the door
did I realize that it was the hallucination of
illness, and even then my consternation was so
great as to deprive me of all power to act or
speak.

The paroxysm soon passed. Meanwhile, I
had poured some brandy into the cup of my
pocket-flask, and offered it to him. He drank

it with a feverish eagerness. By degrees the stimulant seemed to overcome his nervous apprehension. He sat for a long time with listless, leaden eyes. Then he rose wearily and asked, in a humble, deprecating fashion, if there were any place where he might sleep that night.

There was something so piteous, so unutterably wretched in this appeal, coming from one whose wonderful discourse had so delighted me, that I was indescribably touched. " Surely," said I to myself, " such abilities as I have recognized this night shall not be without shelter." I instantly placed my bed at his disposal. After much remonstrance and reluctance, I, at last, got him to bed, and he laid himself down with a long, low, agonizing sigh—the sigh of one to whom life is weariness and existence a burden.

As I stepped to the table near which he had been sitting, I observed a small tin box, something like a tobacco-box, lying in his empty chair. I picked it up mechanically. Such a singular odor rose from this box that I was tempted to open it almost unconsciously. It was half full of a grayish brown drug. I examined it curiously. *Opium !*

I glanced toward the bed. He was lying

apparently in a heavy sleep. I closed the lid
of the box and placed it quietly beside him.
Full of conjecture for the past of the unfortunate being who occupied my bed, I wrapped
myself in my blanket and lay down beneath
the window. There was no sound in the quiet
night save the occasional long howl of the
coyote from the hill. For a long time I lay
awake, pondering over the singular conversation
of the evening and its startling *dénouement.* I
wondered if his hallucination could be directly
traced to opium, and what strange misfortune
could have placed him under the thrall of the
deadly drug. And then my thoughts recurred
to his quotation from Macaulay—" But we know
that there are remedies that will assuage pain."
What was the pain, or what the sorrow?

Unconsciously in my long reverie I had
turned toward him. He was sleeping peacefully in the wan light. The pale moon, looking
coyly over the crest of a western divide, stole
through the files of sentinel mesquites in a long
pencil, and rested like a ghostly arm upon his
breast. I thought, " The sister of Apollo has
him in her keeping;" and I fell asleep. But
in the morning, the hands folded upon the

breast were pulseless and cold; the face was waxen and still; and, hushed in the fearful calm of life's great mystery, *the old man eloquent was dead.*

THE TEMPERANCE BALL AT BRADY.

—o—

THE times were hard at Brady City. Never within the memory of the oldest inhabitant, it appeared, had there been so little doing. From the briefless office of Judge Natchez—the legal luminary of the Concho Circuit—to the editorial sanctum of the "Weekly Bugle," the universal criticism was that of commercial inactivity and financial dullness. "A disheartening paralysis of the local industries, attended with a most deplorable suspension of home credit, is epidemic in our midst," wrote the gifted editor of the latter journal, in that inflated rhetoric with which its readers were familiar. As it was known that the editorial signature, in common with those of all former bibulous patrons, had been recently erased from the credit-slate of the "Morning Call Saloon," this melancholy comment was currently supposed to have a narrower personal bearing.

But of the truth of the editorial dictum there was no question. The five small shops which comprised the "local industries" of the rising town of Brady wore an air of abandonment and desertion. There was an unwonted gloom at the saddlery, and an atmosphere of neglect about the two groceries that ministered to the famished capacities of its citizens. The musical clink of the blacksmith's anvil was rare and intermittent. Even the judgment of Mr. James Wily, that keen student of frontier taste and character, was at last in error. The attractive edifice which, in the interests of his profession and a refined æsthetic taste, he had reared to the goddess, Chance, stood closed and untenanted. The fascinating wheel of fortune, that had so delusively lured the ingenuous sympathies and hard-earned dollars of the inhabitants of Brady in the pursuit of suddenly acquired wealth, withheld its customary whirl. The seductive billiard table, brilliant with mahogany and mother of pearl, that had once proved so irresistible to the casual visitor, stood draped and silent before the gilded bar, and affected the disconsolate proprietor as might the presence of an enshrouded corpse. And the ruined speculator himself—after many efforts to alleviate matters by a judicious display of "free lunches and fancy drinks" in his palace—was constrained to abandon the scene of his financial losses with a depleted pocket-book and a damaged reputation.

It will be seen, too, that this commercial stagnation was alleged to have its origin in social reform. Brady City had recently experienced a temperance revival. The wave of popular enthusiasm that had borne the most prominent of its citizens out of the depths of alcoholic melancholia into the shoals of "Total Abstinence," had passed on to other, and, haply, more urgent towns, leaving behind it the prosaic record of regretted pledges, broken vows, and the disorganized nerves and irritable tempers that attest the despotism of undue stimulation. The last "horrible example" removed from their midst; the pleading eloquence of the reclaimed inebriate no longer urging them by precept and a brass-band; Brady City was experiencing the pangs of regret, and the dangers of reaction. A feeling, that the recent step toward moral regeneration had been hasty and ill-considered, was beginning to possess the despondent community.

" Many things contributed to bring about this yer disgraceful state of things;" apologètically explained Jed Smalley, a reclaimed votary of Bacchus, to the astounded stage-driver who had stopped at the "Hotel" for his customary refreshment—" they jest ketched us between sheriff elections and snake stirrin' in the spring. They wasn't any votin' to be done; the rattlers was all under ground; thet mistake o' the bar-keeper of the ' Two Brothers,' along o' confusin' powdered sugar for cocktails with the *strickenine* he bought for killin' coyotes, hed a depressin' effect on the old soakers; an' altogether Brady whisky seemed to be a drug in the market. Then ole Joe Ferguson he ' had 'em agin',' and was liable to be took bad reg'lar and afore folks, and them temperance sharps, they jest ketched onter him to onct as a shinin' speciment of ' Rum done it.' It was too much for the boys, and this yer town hez been de-looged and drown-*ded* with cold water ever sence."

Nor was the reclaimed Jedediah alone in his despondent opinion.

" I hold," remarked Jackson Sands to a travel-ing drummer in the rear room of his grocery, tapping a large hogshead impressively to enforce

his proposition,—" thet a leetle o' this yer stuff
are pow'ful in cementin' trade and strikin' a
bargain.   It war useless to attempt any bizness
on the frontier 'ithout a nip now and then, jest
to limber up like, the wheels of honest and
fa'r dealin'.   It stimmerlates the acquisition of
goods and chattles, and relieves the stringency
of the money market.   The bottom hez dropt
out of groceries, my friend, sence the recent
crisis."

The Sheriff, also, who, in the unaccustomed
leisure that had overtaken him in the discharge of his usually arduous duties, had
dropped in upon the proprietor for a short call,
added his testimony to the general commentary.

" I tuck down my six-shooter from the nail
where it's been hangin' ever sence this cyclone
of cussed foolishness concluded to strike this
yer unfortunet settlement, and I'm a jack-rabbit,
ef ther wasn't an inch o' rust and vardygrease
all 'round the caps.   There haint been a row or
a spree for the last month thet I've hed any
chance to take a hand in.   Even the cow-boys
hev got it ! I was up in Menard last week at thet
hangin', an' I stopped at Yoho's ranch.

'Wot's up?' sez I, observin' them engaged in brandin'. They hed a large S. O. T. on the side of the nearest heifer. I supposed they war amusin' themselves with the critter, and I larfed accordin'. But I reckon ther wasn't a kid mor'n so high but could hev kerried me back hum without a *habus coppus* when they said them *cows* was now all '*Sons of Temperance.*' It's my opinion, thet ef this yer brain-softenin' continners, it's high time, gentlemen, fur a loonytic commission to set on the inhabitants of this yer county."

Upon a community so circumstanced and commiserated, the darkness of a dreary spring day was now closing in. A northerly gale had been working its exasperating will upon distressed humanity since early morning—rattling the windward shutters and casements, harrying rickety barns and outbuildings, charging the patient stock whose monotonous bells gave the single, narrow street the ludicrous suggestion of a junk emporium, and bullying the unfortunate wayfarer with a pertinacity that provoked the usual profanity.

And, indeed, the condition of the roads made such license not altogether unpardonable. Mud

beset the trails and choked the wheels of pro-
gression throughout the Brady Valley—not the
ordinary complacent and self-satisfied mud that
infests the highways in early spring—but an
uncompromising, **aggressive,** and ambitious
mire that aspires to the qualities of molasses
and glue—mud that rolls up under the boots of
the pedestrian and demands recognition—mud
that is determined to get on in the world
whether he does or not, and, to that end, plays
perpetual " cut behind " with the floundering
legs of the struggling wayfarer—the genius and
abiding despotism of Mud.

Supper was just over at the forlorn " Hotel "
where the varied talent of the little settlement
was wont to repair for rest and refreshment.
The weary lodgers, having disposed of the customary ration of scorched "sow-belly" and
chrome yellow biscuits, settled themselves
about the open fire-place in the " office," which,
in the absence of alcoholic refreshment,
held out a feeble and vicarious consolation to
the outer man. All chewed tobacco and ex-
pectorated violently from morbid sympathy.
A few of the more philosophical took additional refuge in smoking. Indeed the prospect

was in no sense cheering or exhilarating. No
print or gayly colored lithograph illuminated
the blank walls over which the solitary kerosene
lamp shed a flickering and uncertain gleam. A
leaky tin wash-basin and frouzy brush and
comb, that imposed upon the present company
some semblance of the virtue of tidiness, hung
as if in faint protest upon the opposite wall.
A dirty towel, bearing upon its face evidences of
undue familiarity with the features of its last
patron, depended from a nail in the corner.
Meanwhile the wind, increasing in fury with
the approach of night, renewed its boisterous
aggression upon the shaky tenement. At
times a wayward gust, making a burglarious attempt by way of the chimney, swept down and
brightened the embers of the fire. There it
surprised the most prominent of the society of
Brady. Four citizens, already alluded to, were
among those present—the Judge, Jed Smalley,
the Editor, and the Sheriff.

They had been sitting around the fire in
every attitude of complete and irremediable
dejection—the Editor, perhaps, the most shattered and disconsolate of the group. They
were moody, peevish, and distraught. The

subject of their thoughts and meditations was the all-absorbing but depressing theme of Temperance.

Every expedient within the ingenuity of the circle had been resorted to, to dispel the gloom to which hard times and a dearth of spirits conspired. 'Jed Smalley, who had recently returned from a trip to Austin, had regaled his auditors with a lengthy description of a banquet he had attended where "there was seven different styles of drinks—all settin' 'round each feller's plate in different colored glasses. And I settin' thar," added Jed, with grim irony—"passin' myself off fur a temperance advocate, and otherwise doin' the holy horror bizness."

As the staple liquor at Brady had been confined to "40-rod whisky," retailed in beer-mugs, a flattering appreciation of the phenomenal character of Jed's forbearance pervaded his audience.

"They's an Englisher down thar," continued Jed, "hez invented a new kind o' drink, he calls a 'pick-me-up'—the vartues of which, after a mild racket, they allow to be tremenjus. He warrants it to lift a feller quietly out o' bed, put on his clothes fur him, and land him down stares with an appeytite fur breakfast."

The astonishing efficacy of this beverage provoked some interest and curiosity among his auditors.

Hereupon, Judge Natchez excited some feeble merriment by ringing up the bilious proprietor and ordering "extra dry champagne" for every body present in a large and munificent manner, and then countermanding his absentmindedness. But even this ironical tribute to a gilded past lost somehow its power of diversion.

Then the conversation degenerated into personalities.

"The editor of the 'Menard Boomerang' allows that they didn't shet you off 'n yer licker none too soon, Buck," said the Sheriff, quietly raising his eyes from the revolver he had been oiling by the light of the fire, and addressing the representative of the "Bugle." "He sez he's seen traces of alcoholic mane-yer in yer editorials, ever sence thet 'Snake Leader' o' your'n ye wrote last spring."

As the article alluded to was a facetious one upon the alarming increase of the rattlesnake in the frontier counties, the sarcasm was not without its effect upon the Editor.

"Any one engaged, like thet Menard idjit, in editing waste paper, devoted to cow-brands and 'patent outsides,' is not morally or mentally responsible for his vagaries," returned the journalist loftily, rising and knocking the ashes from his pipe, and repairing to his overcoat with an excited, nervous manner that had increased since he had forsworn the "flowing bowl."

The eyes of the assembled company followed him with a singular fascination that could only be ascribed to preconcert of some kind.

As the editorial hand plunged into a side-pocket, in search of the coveted "natural leaf," a huge rat sprang from its recesses, scampered across the floor, and after several attempts to escape, disappeared in a hole in the hearth-stone. The Editor recoiled with an oath and a sudden pallor.

"Did ye see thet rat, boys!" he exclaimed, turning to the group by the fireside with tremulous eagerness.

"Who said anythin' about a rat? What rat?" returned various members of the company.

"Why, thet rat thet jest jumped out o' my pocket? Didn't ye see him? Big as a jack-rabbit and grayer than a badger—ran right over those delicate feet of the Judge's," said the Editor, endeavoring to screen his anxiety under the guise of facetiousness.

"How long is it, Buck, sence you've agreed to 'touch not nor to handle'?" inquired the lawyer with a provoking wink at his auditors.

The journalist's face paled visibly with dreaded apprehension.

"Oh! come off, Judge!" he returned rather feebly, and with a restless hand clutching his scraggly beard, as he recognized the reluctance of the rest of the company to acknowledge his recent visitor—"there *was* a big rat in my pocket—ran right over my hand when I reached down for my plug o' terbacker—a big feller—long ez thet 'Deranger' o' Jed Smalley's. I thought he hed me bit thar! Why what's gone with you feller's eyes?"

But here the excited Editor was met by a dry comment from the practical Smalley—a frontier philosopher in his way—who brought to the settlement of every emergency the test of hard common sense.

"Wotever's gone with 'em, Buck, we'd be certingly better off without any, than to be fashionin' stray snakes, an' rats, and sich like varmin ez them optics o' your'n is continner'ly springin' on an unsuspectin' community."

A roar of approval greeted this sally. Whereupon the man of letters—deserted by his assembled companions, and despairing of support—turned a sharp corner.

"Well, you fellers *are* mighty easy taken in," he said, forcing a ghastly grin upon his pallid countenance. "Did ye reckon I really did see anythin'? I was foolin' yer. *Ther' wasn't any rat!*"

Whereat a chorus of laughter so loud, so shrill, so derisive, and sardonic, disclosed the poverty of the subterfuge, and proclaimed the double humiliation of a detected falsehood and a successful practical joke.

The company had barely recovered from the outburst of merriment into which the recent incident had thrown them, when the sound of hoof-beats outside, and a sharp "Whoa!" announced a new arrival. The creaking door opened suddenly, and a tall figure, projected by the roaring blast behind it, like a bolt from a catapult, shot forward into the room,

It was a figure well known in Brady—the broad shoulders, sturdy limbs, and strong features, almost Semitic in their sallow thoughtfulness, revealed Ebenezer Wilkins, the most popular ranchman in Concho Co.

" Is thet you, 'Snoozer'? " exclaimed Judge Natchez, making use of a popular parody upon the new comer's Christian name, and shifting slightly upon the rough bench for his accommodation.

" What there is left of me ! " returned the figure, stalking gloomily to the fire—" but as near as I can get to it without muscular profanity—that isn't much ! Do you have these blows regular in Brady, or is this one made to order by an outraged Providence for a town where an honest traveler can't beg or steal a drink? "

A groan from the benches testified that he had struck a tender chord.

" Well, how are ye, 'Snoozer,' my boy? " reiterated the legal gentleman, gracefully waiving the recent shaft and answering for the rest. "We ain't sot eyes on you for an age ! "

" About as well as a man *can* be who hasn't

been on speakin' terms with his stomach for the last ten days," returned "Snoozer" gloomily, bestowing a copious baptism of nicotine and a hypocritical grimace upon the hissing coals by way of attesting his alarming physical condition. " I rather allowed to come up here and brace up by a change of diet."

" Reckon ye won't get nothin' but sawdust then," returned the Sheriff, who had desisted from oiling his weapon and now slipped it in its holster—"ye may not know it, my boy, but the town of Brady is a busted community—a reg'lar stampin' ground for jack-rabbits, professional dead-beats, and bummers!"

A dead silence followed this scathing commentary.

" I learn, " finally observed Mr. Wilkins—punctuating his discourse by renewed expectoration upon the coals, expressive of a fine contempt—" thet a band of escaped idjits have struck this yer town, feebly disguised as temperance reformers ; that the poppylation of this village hez riz, and with one fell swoop taken away from an enlightened community the most priceless gift of a free and undivided republic—the privilege for which our ancestors fit, and bled, and died—the freedom and consolation of the social glass ; that the hull community hez been kerflummuxed by a tornado of reform, and,"—he added with withering sarcasm—"thet the only comfort left to a white man is thet he is not included among its citizens."

This severe arraignment was received by his audience in the same stony silence.

After a few moments of pensive and gloomy meditation, the self-constituted mentor resumed :

"What I hev just obsarved is 'hearsay' only, and I trust not to be relied on by any reasonin' bein', but from the general shiftlessness of this crowd," he added darkly, throwing his eyes about him, "I hev my suspicions that 'Mr. R. E. Morse' hez been among ye."

"And suppose," remarked the Editor nervously and avoiding the suddenly concentrated gaze of his auditor—"ye find this yer report to be a fact—what personal criticism hev you got to make !"

"What personal criticism!" echoed "Snoozer," in unfeigned disgust—"none, sir !—none whatever, sir ! To a community thus flyin' in the face of Providence, and blightin' the breath o' trade, I hev nothin' to say. It's beyond me to do the subject justice."

He rose to his feet with a gesture of throwing up a bad hand at cards.

"But," remarked the Editor, growing bolder, as if inspired by the sound of his own voice— "suppose the harm bein' done—what remedy do you propose?"

"What remedy!" replied "Snoozer" with renewed solemnity, gazing thoughtfully around the dejected circle,—"Wal, a quiet, orderly, and thorough application of the art of modern suicide is about the only remedy that I allow to quite fit the urgency of the present crisis. When men git thet beside themselves thet they go to work in cold blood to take away the blessin's provided for alleviatin' the hardships of the frontier, there isn't but *one* remedy. Let every man take his six-shooter and walk quietly out of town as ef he was goin' on a little *pasear*. It spares the town the expense of onnecessary burial, keeps the buzzards busy, and saves the coroner any trouble with his verdict."

"Your treatment of the situation is heroic and self-sacrificing, but not likely to become popular," remarked the Editor with dignity.

"The suggestion which we require from you is something **that** will alleviate the present despondency."

"Well **then, I** should think a ball—a real. live temperance ball—one of them soul-stirrin', maddenin', dissipated 'tears', with refreshments of hard tack and 'lemming soda', is about **what you** require," said "Snoozer" **with** ill-concealed sarcasm. "And I trust you may **all** hev the strength o' soul to resist the temptations of the occasion," **he** added with gloomy irony.

"Gentlemen," **said the** Judge, turning to the company suddenly with that persuasive and convincing manner which was so telling with local juries—"your floor-manager presents you his good wishes for the coming festivity."

And even by this subtle stroke was the project started, and amid deafening cheers and the wildest enthusiasm, the Temperance Ball at Brady was successfully inaugurated.

Late that night, after much exciting discussion and comment, Mr. Wilkins **drew the** Sheriff into a side-room—it having been decided **that** this officer should act as his assistant in the duties of floor-manager—and pinning that small individual against the wall in the grasp of his muscular hand, addressed him in a sepulchral whisper.

"Ike Mosely, have *you* been fool enough to sign this yer pledge?"

"Look a-here!" retorted the Sheriff, writhing in the gripe of his co-laborer;—"how long hev I been sheriff o' this yer town and county?"

"Three years, I reckon."

"And what's my record?"

"Bang up!"

"Wal then, do you reckon thet the feller thet walked in on Jim White in the back room of the 'Two Brothers,' down at Saby, an' tuck his six-shooters away from him, an' waltzed him into the county jail without eny possy, done thet on vichy or salser apparent? Do ye suppose thet when I raided Jim Wily's 'monte game' in the 'Blue Goose Saloon,' I went into trainin' aforehand on cold water an' sponge bathin' to git my narves steady? No, sir! How do you reckon I done them things? Wal, I allow thet two-thirds was grit, but the other third, 'Snoozer,' was—*whisky.*"

"All right!" said Mr. Wilkins with a sigh of relief, producing a large wicker-flask which he uncorked and handed silently to his companion. "Here's suthin' I laid in over to the ranch last year, when I was down in Austin, because I anticipated a liquor famine. It's prime mess, Ike. Drink hearty, and success to the 'Temperance Ball'."

As if encouraged by the prospective festivity, a new era dawned upon Brady City. That night, the boisterous wind that had bedeviled the settlement intermittently for a fortnight, was stricken into a bewildered awe and quiet. In that suddenly capricious climate, the sun, so long withheld, rose smilingly the next morning upon the level plains, and looked down benignly from an azure and cloudless heaven. The bare branches of mesquite, but thinly veiled in green, exhaled a faint odor, and the humbler vegetation raised its tendrils appealingly in the breathless air. In the quiet, serene atmosphere —all athrob with the warm pulses of the coming spring—nature lay as if adream in the trembling hope of resurrection, and basked in blissful and ineffable calm.

Jed Smalley appears to have faintly realized this and delivered himself accordingly.

"It's jest for all the world, as ef nature had

been on a ' bender ' for the past three weeks, and had ended up with a quiet '*still*,' " he remarked to Judge Natchez with tender and regretful alcoholic reminiscence.

The effect upon the editor of the " Weekly Bugle " was radically different. His rejuvenated emotions took refuge in the composition of unusually metrical prose.

" Muse of the many twinkling feet ! whose charms have filled our citizens with soft alarms ; Terpsichore ! for thee, at length, we're ready, and earnestly invite you up to Brady,"— began a subsequent ambitious editorial, hold. ing in dangerous proximity the genius of Byron and Blivins.

" In testimony of the renewed prosperity which has resulted from the temperance move- ment in our thriving community," continued that article, with a mendacity intended for its effect upon neighboring frontier towns, " it has been decided to hold a temper- ance ball in the Pavilion built by the gen- erous hand of our respected townsman, Mr. James Wily, and dedicated to the entertain- ment of his fellow citizens. As it is intended that this brilliant affair of the frontier season shall be characterized by unusual decorum, cow-boys and sheep-men are requested not to present themselves in any other disguise than that of sobriety. No liquor will be sold on the premises, and gentlemen will be expected *not* to smoke on the floor of the ball-room as formerly. It is announced by Mr. Ebenezer Wilkins and Mr. Ike Mosely, floor-managers, that they have in preparation a beverage of their own decoction known as 'Temperance Mead,' which will sufficiently allay thirst. The well-known ability of these gentlemen is a sufficient guaranty for the perfection of the arrangements. The Brady Post brass band has been engaged for the occasion."

The immediate effect of this extravagant editorial appears to have been palliative of the falsehood with which it began. It was in a sense prophetic. The announcement of a " ball " upon the frontier is, at all times, dangerous to the live-stock interests. But a " temperance ball " was entirely subversive of all order and business method. It was more than a novelty ; it was a phenomenon ; and it provoked the wildest excitement. Had an earthquake visited the " ranges " and " ranches " of the plains, they could not have been left more desolate of humanity. Sheep were left to roam recklessly abroad without their herders ; the cattle "drifted" free. For scores of miles around, men poured into Brady City on horseback. But business, in consequence of this sudden irruption of custom, fairly *boomed*. And the cause of this absurd recklessness and foolish abandonment of capital was woman—, *lovely* woman !—an exotic upon the frontier.

The night of the ball had come. The "Wily Pavilion" was a blaze of light. Within, the Brady Post band—consisting of four brass pieces—in all the pageantry of faded military facings and burnished instruments, glowed from the height of a small, elevated platform upon the numerous assemblage, and their leader— a small, red-faced man—glowed also, but in scarlet rivalry of his orchestra, and wiped his fevered brow. Without, through the dark and gloomy night, a large "prairie-schooner" conveyed, by oft repeated trips, the fair ones of the village from their respective habitations to the chance-consecrated bower of this frontier Terpsichore. Already some of the most celebrated had arrived. Seated upon the uncushioned

benches in a remote **corner of the** ball-room—
as yet unvisited by the fascinating but disquieting members of a dangerous sex—they lingered
an eager and fluttering bevy, and were as critical and communicative behind their fans, and
withal as deadly **in** their way, as the aggressive
contingent opposite, which, heavily spurred
and revolver-belted, awaited in solemn and
awkward expectancy the signal **for the ball** to
begin.

In the midst of this blooming parterre, Miss
Penelope Natchez, the youthful but irresistible
daughter **of** the accomplished Judge—already
a terrific heart-breaker among these equestrian
gallants—lifted **her** head coyly, like **a** wild
verbena among more advanced and complacent
Texan *flora*. **It** was her **first** ball. Miss
"Flo" Brooks, intrenched neatly and simply
in a Galveston toilet, darted superb defiance
with feminine intuition of a possible future
rival. And Miss Clorinda Stebbins, outrageous
and overpowering **in** green and pink, bristled
with envy of both, like **an** extravagant prickly
pear.

Outside the gleaming Pavilion, while all
was thus astir with expectation within, two

men were standing near an unfinished rear-
gallery engaged in conversation.

"What's gone with you, 'Snoozer'?" said
the voice of Ike Mosely. "Ye don't reckon to
peg out, do yer? What do ye mean by sayin'
ye'll stay out here?"

"Shoosh!" replied another voice, unmistakable in spite of its disguise. "Ish besher
off here! Shee besher, tell ye! Danshin'!
Moosick! Ike! tell 'em I'm sick—shuddenly
ill! Don't shay anythin' 'bowsh 'temperansh
mead'! Ike! *I sh-a-y, I-ke!*"

But Ike Mosely was off with an oath of
disgust.

Into the room, heeling heavily to leeward
like a diminutive ship in a heavy gale, rushed
the Sheriff. Passing rapidly to the foot of the
band-stand, he spoke hurriedly to the leader and
wheeled rapidly upon the audience.

"Ladies and gentlemen," he began, bringing
down his flat hand upon the platform, as if to
'take it in charge'—"Mr. 'Snoozer' Wilkins
bein' sick and outside—tuck sudden and immejet, ye understand—hez depootized me to
start this thing, an' I hereby does it." Then
smiling blandly, bending forward like a man

about to take a fatal plunge, and waving his hands with a sudden spread-eagle accompaniment,

" In the name of Concho Co. and the Lone Star State, this Temperance Ball is declared open."

The ball opened forthwith.

How, and with whom the partners danced ; what strange steps were cut by the men whose waltzing at times resembled that of jerky and disorganized marionettes ; how elaborate were the curtsies of the ladies, and with what grace and universal self-denial they accepted the Terpsichorean advances of every careering Centaur, I omit from diffidence, but not without regret. An instantaneous photograph alone could fitly portray the highly thrilling scene. I omit also with equal delicacy, how Mr. "Snoozer" Wilkins, in his efforts to adequately realize the gayety within, succeeded in falling through the flooring of the unfinished gallery in the rear, and, being plucked therefrom by eager and sympathetic hands—after turning around several times gravely upon the floor of the ball-room as if to get his bearings, and exhibiting thereby an elaborate assortment of

shavings and sawdust acquired in his descent—
bore down finally upon Mrs. Judge Treddle and
waltzed with her with a preoccupation of manner that dignified the action as a serious business
pursuit.

After this the "temperance mead" was announced—supper being politely overlooked
with customary frontier forgetfulness.

That the ladies declared against this beverage
from the first, sniffed at it, and rejected it, is
beyond question. That the men hailed it, and
partook, as if it were the ambrosia of the gods,
is equally indisputable. But that, having so
hailed it, and so partaken, they eventually
yielded to its insidious influences, was also soon
apparent.

At this point Miss Flo Brooks declared to
her neighbor that she "reckoned there was
something in that mead" from the first, but when
Buck Blivins asked her for the fifth time that
evening to marry him, entirely ignoring the
near presence of Mrs. Blivins herself, and
within easy hearing of two other highly appreciative young ladies, she was "quite sure of
it."

Miss Clorinda Stebbins hereupon requested

her stepfather—who was attempting a frontier *can-can* with " Kickapoo **Dick**"—to take her home at once—with which request, my knowledge **of that** gentleman in convivial matters compels me to record that he was loth to comply. And when Mr. **Rube** Smart absently drew his " six-shooter " from his belt and shot out the top light **in** the ball-room, the entire feminine bevy agreed with Miss Brooks.

But if diffidence restrains me from detailing the early events of that memorable evening, how can I bring myself to paint the developments after the ladies had retired. Indeed the proceedings were of so hearty and sincere a character that I deemed it wise myself to retire at an **early hour.** And if I may judge from the perforated exterior of the whilom abode of Chance the next morning, and the suggestive confusion that reigned within, there was a commendable prudence in my decision, to say the least. I am assured, however, by a friend, who was not so prudent, and who points with singular pride to a bullet-wound indicative of the effect **of** "temperance mead" **upon a frank** and demonstrative nature, that there was a candor and directness about the festivities which, in frontier life, I have witnessed on other less noteworthy occasions. There appears to have been an impression at first that the musicians had not reached that point of exaltation which was deemed fitting and proper under the circumstances; and with the aid of a gallon tin measure, repeatedly filled and generously proffered, they succeeded so well in achieving that point, that the music grew fainter and fainter, until a rotund gentleman, who resided within an equatorial trumpet, with a general suggestion of encircling himself with melody, eventually succumbed, and falling from the platform, rolled upon the floor, where he lay an interesting wreck within his brazen periphery.

At this point the music ceased, and deeds began. There was a pleasing torch-light parade—ostensibly in derision of the temperance movement—highly edifying to the spectator, and apparently enjoyed by those who participated. Certain groups, in remote corners, still pursued the mazes of the dance, assisted evidently by some sublunary orchestra known only to themselves. And strolling listlessly about, a few more abstracted and lonely revelers put out an occasional lamp or lantern

with a target practice that was diligent and unremitting.

And it was at about this witching hour of this
genial frontier revel—the ball-room being only
lighted by a single sputtering lamp—that Mr.
Buck Blivins, leader of the rank and file of the
ironical temperance column—highly excited
and diffuse with his potations, encountered an
unknown figure in the dim light and near the
doorway. He immediately recoiled with a surprise that was caromed forcibly down the reeling line.

"Is thet you—you bloomin' Menard ink-
slinger?" he inquired, in amazement.

"I reckon!" came slyly from the doorway.

"Wal, then, git ready, for now's yer time to
be lookin' out fur *traces o' alcoholic mane-yer !*"

A feeble and wavering six-shooter was instantly raised, and what appeared to be an
effort to bombard both sides of the Pavilion
immediately occurred.

Its effect was instantaneous. In vain Judge
Natchez, with commendable courage, sprang
toward the two men with a threatening gesture
and a voice of remonstrance. The last light
vanished, snuffed by a wandering bullet from

the editorial hand. Column, dancers, and strollers, as if by preconcerted signal, sank to the ground, and amid Stygian darkness a wild and delightfully indefinite skirmish at once began.

Strange to say, no one was killed. For fifteen minutes there was much shooting, abundant smoke, and considerable impotent effort to improvise a barricade of empty benches. A breathless silence ensued. Then a general stampede—more or less protracted during the next half hour from various emergencies. But that Providence which seems to guard the inebriated imbecile was present even here.

Several men were seen around town the next morning with bandaged arms and halting limbs. For some weeks there were a few interesting invalids and crippled "transients" to be seen in the "Morning Call Saloon," which had again somewhat hazardously resumed its credit-slate to a certain spasmodic custom. And Jed Smalley alleges that the Editor, whom he stumbled over, crawling in crippled and serpentine picturesqueness from the Pavilion at an early hour of the morning, had only *one* bullet hole in his back, and this he regarded as a kindly

memento of the precautionary tactics of the
" Menard Boomerang."

But perhaps the true frontier attitude on
" Total Abstinence" was conveyed by Mr.
James Wily in a remark professionally delivered six weeks later. He had been leaning
over his polished mahogany bar, conspicuous
among his highly gilded mirrors and colored
glasses by the absence of coat and collar, and
smoking a huge border Havana at an astronomical angle that probably indicated the
point to which his fortunes were now tending.

Below him the polished ivory spheres shot,
and smote one another musically. The wheel
of fortune had its throng of worshipers, and
about a green table, ominous for certain paste-
board studies in red and black, was the usual
cluster of awe-struck faces.

The eyes of the proprietor were speculative
and dreamy. They were recalled to practical
considerations by the entrance of the Sheriff.

" I'll allow ye don't reckon to interfere with
this satisfactory state of things, Ike?" remarked Mr. Wily, setting out his largest
decanter.

" Wal, no! p'r'aps not—seein' you're slingin'

so much style, and doin' sich a 'nice, clean business,'" responded Mosely with a humorous twinkle.

"What's become o' the 'Snoozer'?"

"Wal, ye see," said the Sheriff, tossing off his liquor—"he hed so much pussonal attention directed to him along o' introducin' thet temperance bev'rage o' his'n, an' bein', as it were, laid out afore it got in its work on the majority, thet he's retired from public life for the present, an' is herdin' all alone by hisself over on the Big Brady."

"Humph! he needn't 'a' done thet!" replied Mr. Wily incredulously—"I set him down fur bein' jest naturally the peartest feller I've struck. *Look at them billiards! See thet 'Monte lay out'!* I tell you, Mosely, it's nothin' short of a miracle, and the only good *I* ever seen come out of a temperance movement."

THE END.

www.ingramcontent.com/pod-product-compliance
Lightning Source LLC
Chambersburg PA
CBHW020856020726
47497CB00005B/1433